Everyday
Miracles

Everyday Miracles

An A to Z Guide to the Simple Wonders of Life

Prartho

Kensington Books
http://www.kensingtonbooks.com

Grateful acknowledgment is made to the following for their kind permission to use quoted material which appears in this book. We have made every effort to obtain permission to reprint material and to publish proper acknowledgments. We regret any error or oversight:

The words of J. Krishnamurti as appearing in *Meeting Life,* and *On Living and Dying,* courtesy of Krishnamurti Foundation Trust, Brockwood Park, Hampshire, UK.

The words of Osho as appearing in *Walking in Zen, Sitting in Zen, Tantra: The Supreme Understanding, The Mustard Seed,* and *The Goose Is Out,* courtesy of © Osho International Foundation.

The words of Jelaluddin Rumi as appearing in *Like This, Birdsong,* and *Open Secret,* courtesy of Coleman Barks, translator.

The words of Deepak Chopra as appearing in *The Way of the Wizard,* copyright 1996, Crown Publishers, Inc.

The words of Antoine de Saint-Exupery as appearing in *The Little Prince,* © 1943 and 1971 by Harcourt Brace Jovanovich, Inc.

"Mother's Day Poem," courtesy of Sumanas.

"The longing for truth" poem, courtesy of Sw. Visarjana.

"Do you think it's possible?" poem, as appearing in the unpublished manuscript *The Rice Washer,* courtesy of P.P.

KENSINGTON BOOKS are published by

Kensington Publishing Corp.
850 Third Avenue
New York, NY 10022

ISBN 1-57566-260-4

First Kensington Trade Paperback Printing: March, 1998
10 9 8 7 6 5 4 3 2 1

Printed in the United States of America

Contents

This book is dedicated to all of you
who play parts, big and small,
in the miracles
that make this dream worth living . . .

but especially to Osho,
my life's greatest miracle,
who once suggested
I might have made him up.

ACKNOWLEDGMENTS

I would like to express my heartfelt thanks to everyone who helped bring this book from seed to flower. All who listened, read, laughed, wept and encouraged. Especially:

Those who helped with early weeding— Abhi Hudson, Alicia Hirshhorn, and Satya Priya.

My agent, Sheree Bykofsky, for her unwavering affection and enthusiasm.

And Tracy Bernstein at Kensington Books whose elegant editing coaxed out the final blossom.

Prologue

I used to keep my photographs in tidy, chronologically ordered scrapbooks. It gave my life a sense of order. It made the ground feel solid beneath my feet.

Then the earth broke open. In the span of three and a half years, I experienced the deaths of both my parents, the births of both my daughters, and the ending of my ten-year marriage. And so I stood with my husband (who was, strangely enough, my best friend through all this) at the edge of the mammoth hole this life-quake had left, while agreements were drawn, possessions were divided, and in a final gesture of fairness, the photographs were divided, too.

For a short while, having been assigned the albums themselves, I carted around large scrapbooks with gaping holes in the chronology. At last, after several moves and coming to accept The World of Shifting Sands as an unexpected but not so horrible home, I dismantled the books and threw them away. The photographs were then somewhat carelessly tossed into a large lidded box. This reduced both weight and volume, and by that time I didn't care about losing the order.

Here's the strange thing: That box of scrambled photos became a box of small miracles. On gray days the girls and I would dive into the box and pull out a snapshot—one moment caught in time. Then we'd dive in and take another, never knowing where we'd find ourselves next.

I came to see that we entered the pictures better this way. Each one came to us fresh, as a moment unto itself—and I have come to suspect that this is the only way to live one.

Out of context, the photos were richer. We took less for granted. We saw deeper into the captured moment, noticing the colors and shapes of the clouds, the angle of light from the sky. Sometimes we remembered the sand beneath our feet— how soft it felt.

I have heard the sages say that we impose time on reality. I have even heard it said that all events are simultaneous. All the moments that ever were, or ever will be, are living together in a great box labeled "Here and Now": all the yearnings, all the fulfillments, all the blood, sweat and tears in between.

It is just that the heart likes stories. So it has persuaded the mind to create Time, a medium in which the unfolding can be watched.

Back in the living room, when it was time to put away the box, the new moment before us was always brighter. We had been reminded to wake up, shake off the past and have a look. Perhaps this is all we ever need to remember.

Our subject is miracles. Not big ones like statues crying saltwater tears, or the moon writing words in the sky. But the little ones that come up in what we affectionately call "the thick of it." Moments when all things stay in their usual places, but the message is shatteringly clear: Compassion is all over the place—in the very air we breathe, if we cease our running from it and enter this moment—the only one there is.

This is a collection of the ordinary stuff of life—pebbles, driftwood and feathers. A brief encounter with a stranger; idle moments watching out a window; conversations while taking a walk; a few dream fragments.

I have not organized my life stories chronologically, but rather alphabetically. This feels most true to our subject. After all, wasn't it learning the dates in history that made it so boring? And isn't there something warmly magical in the alphabet?

Secretly, I have always suspected that the alphabet is the remnant of an esoteric Mystery School. As a child who greatly loved alphabet books, it seems I was on to it at an early age. Yet my suspicions didn't crystallize until I began watching *Sesame Street* with my toddlers. The show, which airs on public television, has no commercials, but instead is "sponsored" each day by a different letter and number. An *S* advertisement, for example, would parade a multitude of *S* words across the screen.

Curious. The words starting with a particular letter seemed like friends and relatives to one another. The *H* words: health, heart, happy, home . . . all had a feeling of warmth and well-being. Also, experimenting with the sound of *H*, I noticed that it is essentially a sigh—a natural way of relaxing, letting go.

Exploring the mystery of *H* with a friend, I pointed out some members of this sighing family: "High, hearth, harmony, heaven . . ."

"Hell," the friend reminded me.

"Hmmmm . . . ," I retreated. (And hurt and harm and holocaust . . .) But, in a strange way, the appearance of these exact opposites in the *H* (and other) families seems only to strengthen the theory. Perhaps, as we all feel at our more inspired times, everything is really round and whole: think of the yin/yang wheel, or the moon with its dark and light sides embracing each other, completing one another. Perhaps in jumping full steam into *H* and finding ourselves on her dark side, we can see what light and darkness bring to a thing. Perhaps in viewing the whole planet of *H*, we may learn something about how the dark cyclone of fear can twist things that begin with warmth and ease.

So here is an adult alphabet book; something I have found missing in my life. A grown-up book of sound, seducing us back to the subtle meaning of utterance—meaning that is not decoded in the brain, but felt in the skin or in the rhythm of the heart.

You will find a "sounding exercise" for each chapter in which I invite you to participate fully. Use your throat and your tongue, your lungs, teeth, lips and belly. In playing with sound, you may find yourself back at the age of innocence when you were just putting your toes into the ocean of language. You might even remember what a miracle each word is.

Despite its appearance, this is not a scrapbook of life stories, but a box. It is meant to be read in whatever order you like: You can let the book fall open, or choose a *"lettre du jour."* What is most important is that while you explore one story, you forget everything you have ever read either in this book or in any other. This way we might really feel how soft the sand is beneath our feet, and we might remember to live our next moment just like this: letting go of all others.

"Remember" was Gautama Buddha's last word to the world. In Buddha's native tongue, Pali, it's an *S* word, like sweetness and sadness and silence: *Samasati.*

A: *Aloneness*

*The great swan
on the wing;
the flight of the alone
to the alone.*

—Zen haiku

Funny we should find ourselves here: at the beginning—alone.

Remember as we enter the alphabet, we may be entering the secrets of a lost Mystery School. Naturally the first secret is of being alone.

Alone: listen to its sound—the ah *bringing us down into our throat; the* l *reassuring us (as the L's do in lovely, lyrical and light) that it's all right to go on; and then the* own *howling like a wolf in the night.*

We could use it as a mantra, a meditative sound: Let the ah *bring us into the throat, the keeper of truth. Bring the tongue to our lip for an* l*—quick reminder never to take anything too seriously. Now, let the* own *take us farther into the belly of our being where the sole, clear voice speaks to us . . . and from which, strangely enough, we are always running!*

Aloneness. What does it mean to me? I remember being happily lost in myself as a child. How easily the hours passed in the sandpile, playing in the shallow waters of the lake, or learning to roller-skate in the empty, unfinished basement. Once, after days of unfruitful coaching from my mother and brother, I was left alone with my bicycle on a spring afternoon. And it was there, under the sky, surrounded by birdsong, away from all human interference, that I found my sense of balance and tamed the unwieldy beast.

As an adult I have experienced loneliness, the painful side of aloneness. I have tried to fill up that empty belly of my being and quiet the wolf's howl in thousands of ways. But the strange, lovely haunting continues in spite of everything.

What follows is the story of a day when Aloneness rose and let me look at her, face-to-face:

By late 1979, the gulf between Terry and me yawned wider every day. Marrying one another at the age of twenty-one, we had grown up together; nursed each other through sickness, health and graduate school; had extramarital affairs, confessed and got over them.

We had raised dogs, chickens and babies; painted houses and weeded gardens. We had sung together on Sunday drives, built fires and had long talks over them. We had learned how to make one another laugh; we had cried countless tears in one another's arms.

But some time between our tenth and eleventh anniversary, we came upon the greatest challenge. Dropped from a tornado of deaths and births, two new people looked out at one another. We ate different foods at different times, went with different people to different places, and gradually spoke different languages.

During that year of growing apart, we made many efforts to reach across the gap. We remodeled the house. We made a baby. We threw the party of our lives.

In a few days we were going to find ourselves in George Orwell's ominous decade. The 1980s had seemed lifetimes away when we read *1984* in our teens, but that dark era, with its clouds of corruption and confusion, was now upon us.

What to do but celebrate? We bought large foil numbers that read 1980 to string across the entrance. We bought hats, noisemakers and food for multitudes. We assembled a large list of guests from our separate corners of the world.

It was I who suggested that we invite Stephanie and her husband. Stephanie, a woman of our age, was Terry's student.

He had confessed to falling in love with her last term, which was not a particularly new story; Terry liked falling in love.

My usual way of dealing with Terry's loves was to meet them with trust, and even welcome them into my life. Thus, I put Stephanie and her husband at the top of our guest list, which was composed, reflective of that time in our lives, entirely of couples.

For most of the last day of 1979, Terry and I were in overdrive, making ready. We worked well together, staying in tune with what the other might need and being quite economical with words. Guests started to arrive around eight o'clock and spread out into almost every corner of our large four-bedroom farmhouse. Some couples meandered around and explored the rooms, where we had taken out three layers of ceiling to expose the original beams, or where I had painted murals on the bedroom walls. Some couples separated into small male and female groups, and there was a very lively kids' room where I found myself much of the early evening.

Around eleven o'clock Terry and I found each other and decided to bring everyone together in the living room for a game of charades. The pantomimes brought much laughter, and time passed swiftly.

Somewhere on our journeys together Terry and I had acquired an antique, windup clock that chimed out the hour. We kept it on the newly constructed mantelpiece in the living room. When I looked up at the clock and noticed that we were approaching midnight, I pulled out the box of noisemakers and hats and began to distribute them. As I became absorbed in a game of finding the right hat for the right face, I lost track of the time.

The old clock on the mantel took me by surprise with its first gong! There was an uproarious chorus of noisemakers and shouts, and then everyone in the circle turned to his or her mate and kissed. I was standing in the middle of the room, the clock chiming, and I turned to find Terry for our New Year's kiss, as I had turned to find him for eleven other New Year's kisses.

But as my eyes found him, I froze, and the moment became huge and silent. Many people speak of this expansion of time and space when they are in an accident: When everything has gone out of one's control, time stops and with it, strangely enough, so does fear.

Time and fear gone, things spread out. The accident itself becomes an exquisite, slow-motion ballet. In the same way, within twelve gongs of an antique clock, in amazing slow motion, my life took a 180-degree turn.

About eight feet away from me were Terry and Stephanie. The energy that passed between them was an almost visible electric current. They were lost.

Or I was. Like a ghost, I was suddenly in the curious vantage point of being able to witness everything without being noticed.

The first thought that entered my mind: "I am alone."

Suddenly embarrassed, I looked around for someone else who might be without a partner. (Stephanie's husband, for example. I have not, to this day, figured out where he hid himself at midnight.) I found no one else.

There was no escaping, nowhere to go. Terry and Stephanie melted into the circle of other couples. I was still curiously invisible, at the center of the circle—all by myself.

I am alone, I thought again; this time I was in the belly of it.

Now the whole secure world I had been building for eleven years melted, too. As the clock struck its twelfth note, I fell through my howling belly into a gap of immense purity—strangely impersonal, but not altogether unfamiliar. I was at the start of a new game, at the beginning. I had drawn the first card of the tarot deck. I was the Fool.

And when the mind finally recovered enough to speak, it said the words one more time. The voice that now spoke was an old intimate friend. In this moment, all clutter swept away, I heard once again my still small voice: "I am alone."

B: Beauty

*So what is beauty? ... Is not beauty
something that takes place when "you" are not;
"you" with all your problems, with your
insecurity and anxiety as to whether you
are loved or not? When "you" with all these
psychological complexities are not, then
that state is beauty.*

—J. Krishnamurti

Beauty. Dare I speak of it? Isn't the intellect a diesel truck plowing through the cricket song of a summer night? Isn't beauty the room where the mind is not allowed to enter?

Yet, the heart makes its home here. And it is the writer's work to make irresistible overtures to all that exists beyond language. Stringing words together, she makes a sort of wind-harp and waits with hope that the wind might come and make music.

Beauty. Let's enter its sound. Bee-you-tee. (Bernie Gunther, in his book, What To Do Until The Messiah Comes, *breaks the word beautiful into "Be-You-To-Full," which is beautiful in itself; but let's let the sound teach us.)*

B-b-bee ... there is a playful beginning in bee, the way the ee is thrown out from the tucked-in lips. The B alone is pure play (ball, bounce, burp, bing, blam!). Children in that early stage of babble (a word loaded with B's itself!) start many of their words with this sound. It goes well with drool: "Bwee!" I can still hear (and feel the wetness of) my daughters exclaiming, "Bwee!" when sound was their only meaning and they wanted to say something like, "Great! wow! far out!"

When we add the ee, our B is freed: the E-energy has escaped and is flying.

Now eau/you. The sound of "you" is mostly breath. The other nuances of the sound ride on the breeze of it. "You" is a whisper. Have you ever said it to a lover, all by itself? "You . . ." The heart's whole secret is there. There is a softness, awe and willingness in "you."

But we must leave this softness and come to tee. *The lips stretch back, and the tongue taps quickly upon the teeth, making the sharp sound of* t. *It brings us out of our infatuation, like the teacher's pointer stick against our desk. It reminds us that we have a left brain, a male side, a western hemisphere that must be included in our sense of beauty. Without the* T *we might have gotten lost in our sweet imagination. But now, feeling that* T, *we can end our story with one more* ee. *Allowing both Heaven and Earth to sing in us, we are again set free:* Bee-You-Tee. Beauty.

Beauty. Heaven and Earth. Mud and lotus. At what moments in my life did beauty find me? My father on his deathbed, totally bald and bloated from chemotherapy, helpless, unable to move or speak. And yet so open, so vulnerable, so available to us who were near him. To the moment. Even to his own death.

Beauty. What beautiful faces have I seen? The old Mexican woman, wrapped in her blanket, sitting contentedly at the edge of town. The Indian tailor rolling his brightest bolt of cloth across the counter, his eyes full of delight. My one-and-a-half-year-old daughter lost in herself on an ocean beach.

Beauty. Alone at dawn in a bamboo grove. Yosemite Falls in the pouring rain. A cool breeze at the end of a hot day. Heaven and Earth holding hands. And I a little emptier than before.

There is a story about Kahlil Gibran in art school when his drawing teacher said that Gibran had a tendency to make the model too beautiful.

"This is strange," answered Gibran. "I have found that no matter how hard I try, I cannot make her as beautiful as she is."

There is another story, a mysterious one about the relationship between truth and beauty. A friend of mine, who is a professional storyteller, told it to me. He said it was the strangest story to tell because it left everyone silent for a while: There once was a man who passionately wanted to know Truth. His thirst haunted him endlessly until finally he left his wife and family and went on the proverbial pilgrimage in search of Truth. He lived as a beggar, traveling from land to land. At last, his search brought him to Truth—an old woman living in a hut at the edge of a primeval forest.

She had lost all but one tooth, and her skin had become like leather from years of exposure to the sun and the wind. Her hair was thin, gray and wild. She wore a torn, faded cloth wrapped around her body, and sandals that had been mended many times.

Truth received the man warmly. She took him in and agreed to teach him everything she knew. He studied with her long and hard, and grew to love this woman who had the capacity to teach him the living truth of all things.

After many years, it became apparent that it was time for him to leave her, to go into the world and make positive use of what he had learned.

With his satchel at his side, and tears of gratitude in his eyes, he took the hands of Truth and asked, "Is there anything you would have me tell the thirsty people in the valley below?"

"Yes," said Truth with a twinkle in her eye. "Tell them I am young and beautiful."

This miracle is from my childhood.

I was in first grade at St. John the Baptist, a Catholic school. The teacher's name was Sister Mary Something. For the most part she did not make much of an impression on me. Not like my second-grade teacher, Sister Maria Josephi, whose hyena laughter and unsurpassed talent for inventing practical jokes will live in my heart forever.

Sister Mary William (yes, that was her name) was quiet and withdrawn, and each day of first grade with her seemed pretty much like the one before it. But this one day with Sister Mary William, for a few moments at least, I was definitely not bored.

She was teaching the religion lesson and she was talking about Heaven. "They say that Heaven is so beautiful that we cannot imagine it," she told us. "They say it is even more beautiful than this earth . . ." And then she paused for an uncomfortable length of time. I saw tears welling up in her eyes behind her glasses. "And this earth is so beautiful . . . ," she almost whispered.

Maybe I had never looked into the eye of someone who had been touched in a private way before. Maybe that was true for all of us, because I remember a strange, new silence that filled the room as Sister Mary William regained her composure and became boring again.

This must have been the first time I had heard a teacher (maybe anyone) allow something to erupt like that. The rawness of it made me feel as though she were, for a moment, standing there naked.

And the content shocked me, too: The Earth is beautiful? Wasn't something ugly always gaining on us? Wasn't it always too muddy, too hot, too cold, or too gray? Why, even the good days were too short! Even I, a first-grader, could see that something dismal permeated the universe. My young mind was already working on changing what could be changed and learning to endure the rest.

But here was Sister Mary William saying something different. And she hadn't memorized it from her catechism. She actually felt it. She had seen something that my six-year-old eyes were already beginning to miss. But I lived from that day on figuring that it might be possible to see a beautiful world, right here on this, the other side of paradise.

C: *Courage*

༄༅༄

*That is the only courage: to drop the known
and to move into the unknown. And it
has not to be done only once, it has to be done
every moment ...*

—Osho, *Walking in Zen, Sitting in Zen*

A friend recently took *neo-sannyas* initiation, a new version of the ancient Hindu vows of renunciation. Instead of taking vows of poverty and celibacy, the *neo-sannyasin* simply renounces the past: one's history, conditionings and beliefs. The initiation ceremony is a small celebration of the initiate's fresh beginning, which is commemorated by the taking of a new name. My friend was given the name "Saahas" and told that it meant "courage" in Sanskrit.

When I first heard the name and its meaning, I was quite shocked. Why, that doesn't sound at all like my idea of courage! All the sounds are so soft: "S-s-s-Ah-ah-ah-Ha-has."

"There is nothing to hang onto," I complained to my newly initiated friend. "No *T* or *B* or *D* or *M*, no letters with that hard, definite quality. Nothing to sink your teeth into."

This is courage? Where is the brute strength? The lion's roar? This "saahas" seems to contain the courage of a dandelion!

And yet it occurs to me, as I have rolled the word "saahas" around in my head for a few months, that the greatest courage might well be the courage of a flower—standing there so soft and yielding, nondefensive, letting go.

Courage. Let's listen to the story in her sound.
C—we make this sound at the back of our mouth, like a frightened being huddled at the back of his cave. C. It's an animal sound. It

voices our fear of what unknown creature or event might come out of the dark.

So courage begins with fear. Of course. How can there be courage without fear? But we have a choice. We can let the fear overwhelm us, or we can find that little light in the heart that welcomes the unknown.

In our "cow"ardly moments we get lost in fear. We cry, "C-ow!," expressing the pain of being stuck in fear. But the courage in us sings a different song. We move into the sound oor. *The* oo, *a welcoming sound, saying "yes," the* R *at the end of our* oo *giving us* richness. *The Hindi word for gold is* rupee, *the French word for gold is* oR. *The rolled* R *is perhaps the R-richest sound in any language. And so, with this first syllable, "Cour," we seem to be saying, "Let's discover the richness—the gold—of the 'feared' moment before us."*

Now age. *This a sound is one of the first baby sounds. It is pure energy, like* ee, *but softer:* aa. *The* ge *moves the* a *softly out into the world. And so the energy of our golden discovery is expressed: Courage is born.*

A sad young woman walked into my life once and called from me the courage of a flower. In this case, it was a daffodil.

I was a counselor at the Bowling Green State University Counseling Center in Bowling Green, Ohio, when a student was referred to me because she was suicidal. She had made an attempt (slit a wrist) and, thanks to the benevolence of the powers that be, she was allowed to stay in school within several strict parameters. One of these was seeing me three times a week.

This was in the early 1970s when, inspired by Joni Mitchell and others, everybody wore their hair as straight as possible. Some of us struggled endlessly with ironing, straightening solutions and orange-juice cans for rollers, usually to no avail. But her long unrippled hair was perfect for the era, with the added benefit of creating a thick brown curtain behind which she could hide.

When she first walked into my office, all I could see of her face was a nose. She had learned to navigate from beneath her veil of hair by walking at tortoise pace and looking only a few feet ahead. When finally seated, she crossed her legs, folded her hands on her lap and didn't move for fifty minutes. This entrance and the lifeless act that followed were repeated for four sessions.

The physiological psychologists tell us that we use between seven and ten percent of our brains. (As a comparison, rats are reported to use ninety percent!) These psychologists get their data by hooking subjects up to brain-wave equipment and performing complex statistical analysis. Interestingly enough, from a purely subjective point of view, Einstein estimated that, at his best, he was using only ten percent of his brain. This was before the instruments to measure such phenomena had been invented and says a lot for the possibility of subjective knowing. But the main point here is that we have barely skimmed the surface of our intelligence as human beings.

I point all this out because I was just out of graduate school as I sat there trying to reach this young woman, and I figure I was running on about seven and a half percent. I had stuffed my brain with theories and techniques, and in the first three sessions I tried everything I knew. I tried to be Carl Rogers, but that was very difficult, because he reflects back everything the client has said. I would say, "You don't feel like talking . . ." and several minutes later, all I could say was, "You still don't feel like talking."

I tried to be Fritz Perls, who believed in confrontation. Ultimately he would put the person on the "Hot Seat," and if the client had nothing to say, Fritz would leave. I wasn't ready for that.

In the end, I even tried a Freudian approach. Having no input from her, I talked about my own dreams, remembered my own childhood, free-associated about things in my office. She did not respond, but continued to sit behind her hair, unmoving.

By the fourth session, I was exhausted. I fell into that delicious kind of exhaustion where the world of frantic searching stops and the mind simply opens.

I stopped running on my seven-and-a-half-percent mental treadmill and considered: She came to all of our sessions. She was not only on time, she was almost always early. She is here,

I thought. On some level she is willing. If there is a way for one human being to help another, it seems I will have to find it on my own.

So I threw Carl and Fritz and Sigmund out of my office and sat back, listening for the wingbeats of inspiration. I don't think I realized it then, but this was my first courageous step as a therapist. I had untied my boat from the moorings of Other People's experiences and theories. I was captain of my own ship, out to discover my own way.

I turned my chair to look out the window, to gather myself for this voyage into the uncharted. It was February—cold and gray, with no sign of green anywhere. As I gazed into the stark landscape of the university cemetery across the street, an unexpected sensation arose: I smelled daffodils.

It wasn't roses or lilacs or gardenias. It was the very subtle and yet distinct smell of daffodils. In my mind I reviewed passing through the front office. Had one of the secretaries brought in daffodils this morning? But, no. It was February and there were no daffodils anywhere. I knew what to call this; I was a psychologist, after all. This was an hallucination, a figment of my imagination.

The fragrance vanished as quickly as it had arisen. Once it was gone, I turned around to face my frozen companion. By this time, I was used to talking to myself, so I openly mused, "That's funny, I just smelled daffodils."

Now the student pulled aside a curtain of hair and looked at me with one eye. "I didn't know daffodils smelled," she said.

We both stopped.

As I looked into the stranger's eye in front of me, I had to process three shocks before I could say anything. The first shock was that there was someone in there! I had gotten so accustomed to her facelessness. The next shock was that she had responded to this—an hallucination. They didn't teach us anything about sharing our own hallucinations in graduate school.

But eventually I looked into this person's eye and experienced a third, more human shock: Here was a seventeen-year-old girl who was raised in Ohio—where winters are mostly gray and slushy, where spring is a long-awaited explosion into color and life—and she had never bothered to smell a daffodil.

So that's what I finally said. "You never smelled a daffodil? I wonder what else you have missed?

"What else haven't you smelled ... or tasted ... or felt? Have you been in love yet?"

She was still looking at me when I said to her, "You know, I think you should stick around until April and smell a daffodil. Then if you want to leave, okay."

She smiled and hooked her hair around her ear, exposing half her face. She folded her arms across her chest and nodded almost imperceptibly, signaling that she was with me now, and I could continue.

This became her ritual for the next few months: first sitting in my office chair and then hooking one curtain of hair around her ear, folding her arms and nodding. She listened attentively and gradually began responding. Soon we were spending our counseling hours outside, walking among the trees, in the corn-fields, and through the cemetery. She loved the simple details of nature and taught me many things. In early spring I still look for the pink haze of ripe buds on the maple trees before the leaves sprout.

We saw each other three times a week until that spring semester was over. Toward the end of the term, she was walking with her full face in the wind, and frequently brought friends to meet me. During our last session, the office was overflowing with young women, sharing stories and laughter.

This was the end of my stint at the counseling center, so I did not see my sensitive, young friend when she returned to school the next fall. The last I heard from her was a letter that contained a carefully wrapped shell necklace she had strung for me. She was enjoying her summer on the family farm ... and had fallen in love.

It took a long time for me to get a handle on what had happened that afternoon when the daffodil spirit came to visit—why such a strange, simple fluke had opened this closed bud of a woman.

At last I came to trust that someone very wise lives in us. Someone who knows just the right touch for bringing each moment to life. The daffodil was a perfect symbol for what this woman needed. She had given up on relationships and feelings, and the complicated knots these two conspire to tie, but there was still the earth with its renewal and forgiveness—sending up daffodils for no reason, every spring. To speak of daffodils was a brilliant idea. I wish I'd have thought of it!

Some say this peculiar inner voice, which speaks in cryptic phrases, fleeting images, even smells, is the voice of God. There may be some grounds for this: I have heard that for millennia God couldn't get any rest. People were harassing Him endlessly with their petitions for this and that. At last, He came upon a way to manage a little peace. "I'll hide inside of the people," He thought. "Nobody ever thinks to look there!"

It is said that this worked splendidly and that God is well rested these days—not so worn out and crabby as He used to be.

And so it seems that no matter how much it appears to elude us, the Source of Wisdom is never far away. But it cannot reach us when we are running on the squeaky treadmills of borrowed knowledge. It cannot reach us even when we are trying to imitate ourselves. It is only with each courageous step into the unknown territory before us that the voice can be heard. That's why the Inspired Ones call this life an adventure.

D: *Dance*

❦

*I had to clap and sing. I used to be respectable
and chaste and stable, but who can stand in
this strong wind and remember those things?*

—Rumi, *Like This,* Versions by Coleman Barks

Let's begin this one with a story—a story that my meditation
master Osho loved to tell.

There once was a musician in India who was considered a
magician of sound and silence. It was said that even the birds
stopped their singing to hear him play. However, he rarely
played arranged concerts, for he felt that music should be given
at the moment it is felt.

The king of the land, a kindly and wise ruler, heard about
the legend of this man and begged him to give a concert for
the residents of the capital city. To show his goodwill, the king
offered to hold the concert in the palace courtyard.

At first the virtuoso refused, but seeing the good heart of
the king, he eventually consented, adding a very strange and
difficult provision: Anyone who moved visibly during the music
would be beheaded. Of course the king tried to persuade the
musician to soften the consequences of such a small act, but
the artist insisted. Only under these conditions would he play.

And so arrangements were made; tickets were printed with
the condition and consequence clearly written on them. Posters
were made stating the risk involved in attending the auspicious
event. Still, on the appointed evening, hundreds of people
crowded into the courtyard.

All along the walls of the yard stood soldiers from the king's private troop. They stood tall in their regal attire with naked swords upright and ready.

When the musician appeared on the stage, a great hush fell over the crowd. He looked out over them for a long time, and then he lifted his instrument. A heavenly sound filled the air. The musician closed his eyes and fell into a trance, and his music took a dive into the place where all souls meet. All—the king, the musician, the audience and the guards with their naked swords—were lost together in this ocean of sacred song. But at one point, the king remembered his promise to the musician, and opened his eyes to find half of the listeners tapping their feet, bobbing their heads, and swaying in time to the music. The king was horrified and just at that moment, the musician also opened his eyes and shouted, "Stop!"

Now the courtyard was totally still. The musician rose and walked to the front of the stage. "Please point out all those who were moving during my playing," he said to the guards. "And include those among your ranks who also moved. When I opened my eyes, I saw many of the guards also with eyes closed, swaying."

And so the audience and the guards were sorted into two groups: those who had remained still, and those who had not.

The musician said, "Those who remained still may now leave; those who did not will stay here."

Again no one spoke as half the crowd left the courtyard, and the king hung his head in remorse. So many of his most trusted friends (and certainly all the children in attendance) remained.

Now all in the courtyard were as still as statues as they awaited their sentence to be accomplished.

But the musician surprised them all. "At last," he said. "At last I have found the audience I have been looking for all my life: those who enter this music as deeply as I do, who cannot stop dancing even at the risk of losing their heads. . . .

"Let the real concert begin!"

And so we enter the mystery of dance. The spontaneous, rhythmic movement of body, heart and soul when we are touched by music and let go.

What do we find in the sound of Dance?

We begin with d. *In what company do we find ourselves beginning
with* d? *Do, doubt, divide, dash, decide, drum, daddy, dare* ... d *is
a sound acquired early in life; in fact, most English-speaking fathers
brag that their children learn to say "Da-da" well before they are able
to say "Ma-ma." The* d *sound is the energy of action, it is pure will;
with* d *we move out into the world with intent. D: We move onto
the dance floor, strong, able and ready. We embrace the male in us,
the adventurer, the dad.*

*But once on the dance floor, we must allow the feminine with all
her receptivity and willingness to take us:* ance. Aaannn. *We go from
openmouthed* aaa *to the hushed, inner sound of* nnn. a—*the soft,
flatter side of A. A sound that slides in from the side and invites us,
without self-consciousness, to dance.*

N—*makes a strong vibration in the head, especially in the ears.*
N *drowns out all the words, the inner and outer dialogues. Maybe
this is why the two-year-old is so taken with "N-No!" Once again,
he is inside himself.*

So in aann *we enter the female, yin—silent and inner. And with
ce we go soft. We let happen what will happen. Now we are complete.
The inner partners, male and female, have met in the willfulness of
d and the willingness of ance. We are whole. We can dance.*

Dance is one of the great symptoms of life. Where there is
life, there is dance. Raindrops dancing on the lake, birds dancing
in the sky, fire dancing in the night. Dance is as old as the hills;
hasn't the wind always danced there? It is as deep as the sea;
don't whales jump just for the joy of it?

I have danced myself out of sadness, as though it were a
dry old skin. I have watched a room full of dancing strangers
become an intimate tribe.

Dancing turns us liquid. All things solid dissolve in dance:
the static picture of who we thought we were. In dancing we
play at being ourselves instead of working at it.

One morning when I was a cook at a vegetarian restaurant,
I came to work oozing sadness. My cooking partner was Narayana, a large black man whose hair was a mop of beaded braids
and who was variably reclusive and playful. Narayana was
already in the kitchen slicing vegetables when I arrived. He had

put on his favorite reggae music and was dancing to the beat as he sliced. When he saw my face, he stopped.

"What's happened?" he came over to me and asked.

I tried to tell him that my love affair had just ended, but the tears came before I completed my sentence.

Narayana took my hands and began to dance with me to the reggae music. "There's only one thing I've learned in life that gets me through it all," he said. "You just keep dancing.

"Sometimes you have a partner and sometimes you are alone, but you just keep dancing."

I have remembered this bit of wisdom often, but sometimes when my world has really toppled, I forget. This story is about a forgetful moment, and the remembrance.

I was living in a spiritual commune on the West Coast of the United States. I had come three years before to experiment with another way of living—one that encouraged integrity and innocence, spontaneity and joy.

The commune was a micro-global village—a colorful mix of thousands of people of all ages from all over the world. I loved living in this New World city where meditation, celebration, hard work, and a shared love for Osho—the commune's spiritual inspiration—were the glue. Never in my life before or since have I mingled with so many bright, good-humored people, worked so hard (twelve or more hours a day), or danced so long (in whatever waking hours were left before sleep).

Finding myself in this delightful experiment in human relating was miracle enough, but the opportunity to live and learn in Osho's presence was nothing short of my life's greatest blessing.

I had met him five years before, when I went to India to see what I might find in his eyes. Before I left on my pilgrimage, I talked about it to many people, but I especially remember this exchange: "You know all the answers are inside you," one friend reminded me. "Why are you going to meet this *guru*?"

I responded, "His books have made more sense to me than anything I have read or heard from anybody . . . and he is *alive!* I just want to have a look into those eyes and see for myself who's in there."

My friend gave me his blessings, and I set out to test the

waters—to find out if I would be disappointed again or not. You see, I was the childhood agnostic, the one who started doubting in first grade, the one who decided at twelve years old that nobody could be trusted completely, that everybody was pretending in one way or another.

But what I found when I finally sat in front of Osho at my initiation ceremony was one whose presence defied my conclusions. Here was one who sparkled with integrity and innocence, spontaneity and joy. I was awed by his radiance but also afraid. Sitting in that light, I saw all my own pretensions come out of hiding. I was so frightened, in fact, that I squeezed my eyes shut as I waited for Osho to give me my *mala* (beaded necklace, traditional symbol of spiritual initiation) and my new name. But I felt him lean toward me and gently whisper, "Look at me . . ."

When I opened my eyes, I felt so much love coming from his that my fears melted into a strange mix of tears and laughter. As he spoke to me about my journey, describing my most secret disappointments and longings, rocks of petrified emotion continued to dissolve and run down my face.

Because many thousands of us, each in our own way, felt deeply about this man, personal encounters with Osho were rare. But sometimes one of his words or gestures would touch me from a distance—when he lectured from the podium or on a video—and that same tears-and-laughter meltdown would happen. Still, I always hoped that I would have a chance to look directly into those eyes again.

It was a time in the life of the commune that we were to affectionately dub later as "when the shit hit the fan." In spite of the joyful everyday life within the work teams (who were building a model ecological city in record time), the commune's administration, under the weight of both internal and external political pressure, gradually sank into corruption. A moment came when the corruption could no longer be concealed. It was becoming more and more obvious that something was dreadfully off.

Osho's role in the commune was that of nonpolitical, spiritual guide. I think of him as a court jester in the workings of the community—the watchful one who remains outside the bargaining table, making riddles, telling stories, and ultimately trusting in the court to see its own folly. For most of the commune's life he remained basically in silence, speaking only once a day to the community's director. After three years of watching, he took up his evening talks again, and soon began speaking more and more directly about the organization.

When it became absolutely clear that Osho was not in support of the power structure, the group of women who were the commune's coordinators fled in panic. They left without warning, overnight, and not only from the commune, but from the country.

The next day Osho spoke to us about the corruption of the organization. He told us we were all responsible, encouraging us to see how we had contributed to the climate of corruption. This was the exact moment of "the shit hitting the fan."

I was immersed in one of the most difficult learning experiences of my life as I struggled to find the part in this drama for which I was responsible. It brought forth a huge confused body of memories about power struggles and how one cooperates in becoming a victim. I saw replays of how I had cowered and played dumb with my parents, teachers and supervisors, how I had pretended to be a powerless victim because I did not have the courage to stand firm in my own intuitive knowings. I saw that sometimes I even imitated the ones in power.

Eventually I was able to forgive myself and everyone else for not understanding these things right at the beginning. I realized that we had come together as an experiment—to learn from the experience. And eventually I came to see that this experiment helped many of us subsequently find the courage to be true to ourselves.

But first, I was thrown into an ocean of doubt. I doubted everything: the master, the commune, myself. My philosophical take on everything was in shambles. I was back to ground zero.

In this state of psychic ruin I was invited to be one of the forty or so guests who lined the walkway where Osho would pass on his way to evening discourse. I had been a walkway guest twice before. Although this was an everyday event, it was celebrated like a major festival every night. A band of musicians filled the air with music, and the event was studded with breath-taking moments, as Osho would choose a dance partner from time to time as he moved along the line.

I was allowed to leave my job in the commune's welcome center early in order to get ready. As I walked home, my mind was a hurricane of questions: Who was this guy with the magnetic eyes and graceful hands, and what part did he play? What was my responsibility in it? How much did I contribute to the chaos around me now? There were no answers to these questions, and by the time I reached my room, I was mentally exhausted.

I wasn't going, and that was it.

What I usually would have seen as an invitation to a gala event, prompting me to dress in glittery clothes, seemed like one more senseless moment. I changed into old jeans and a sweatshirt, and collapsed on my bed.

No one was in the communal house as the workday was still in progress. I never felt more an outsider in my life. I looked out the window at the trees and at the clouds as they were blown around in the wind. I stayed very still for a long time when suddenly I was "called back."

Without a thought I stood up to go. I put on a large, floppy beret, adding a rather comical touch to my appearance and walked out the door. I walked through the fog of my mind to the bus stop. (Because the ranch we lived on was very large, transportation was provided from one part of the commune to another on yellow school buses.) As if by design, the bus arrived without any wait. I walked from my house directly up its steps and rode silently to the spot where Osho would arrive.

I spoke to no one as I found a place to stand on one side of the path. If nothing else, it will be good to see him, I thought.

Osho's car arrived, and the band of gypsy musicians already gathered there began playing, while colorful ribbons flowed from their costumes and instruments. Osho appeared, and the crowd swelled with excitement. Looking out from my eyes, I felt as though I were miles behind them. I felt as though I were in that ocean of music and dancing, but not *of* it. As he came closer, I watched him with the greatest sense of not-knowing-anything that I have ever experienced. And he saw me.

He was several people away when his eyes caught mine. It felt as though he saw *into* me, all the way back to the miles away where I stood behind my eyes. There was a flash in that moment. My breath stopped. The world stopped. And then my greatest hope and my greatest fear met: his eyes did not leave mine as he walked directly for me.

The band followed him as always. So did the video lights and the video camera, which taped the nightly sessions. In one graceful swoosh he was before me, and the whole world was behind him: lights, music, people dancing ecstatically . . . and all the things in the world beyond that. He and I were together, face-to-face, in a silent bubble.

I have always been a loose free-form dancer, but now I was stiff with doubt and fear. I jumped lightly up and down and, keeping my arms close to my sides, I clapped as he stood right in front of me. He moved his hands up and down vigorously like a great symphony conductor.

I looked into his eyes with all my not-knowing-anything, and fell into them. The closest thing I have seen to what I saw in those eyes was the desert sky on a clear, cool night. I was sure they went on forever, and it was too much for me. I closed my eyes and continued to jump up and down and clap, now with all my heart.

I stayed inside for what felt like an eternity until I finally peeked out to see if he was still there. Not only was he there, but his look was almost fierce and his movements had taken on more passion. It was as though his whole being, and maybe the whole sky, had come to me and were demanding that I "dance"!

I closed my eyes again, and this time my body opened and became a tree dancing in a great wind. My arms were loose and wild. They spoke the unspeakable things that were now stirring inside.

When I opened my eyes again, Osho was still there. This time, there was a hint of a smile on his face. His hands came down in the movement of a sensitive conductor finishing his piece, and he moved on, leaving me dancing.

Now I was no longer a tree but the wind itself. There was a lightness in me, a newfound joy. Life was suddenly simple again. Those fierce eyes had come to remind me that you just keep dancing.

Sometimes you have a partner, sometimes you're alone. Sometimes you think you have a handle on it all, sometimes you don't understand a thing. But you just keep dancing.

E: *Emptiness*

*Methinks that what they call my shadow
here on earth is my true substance.*

—Herman Melville, *Moby Dick*

Emptiness.

The center of the cyclone. The space between breaths. The hurricane's eye.

The stillness before the storm. Silence before the word. Darkness before the dawn.

The bottomless. The unfathomable. Nothing at all.

We come into this world empty. Naked and nameless, without history or identity. We come with nothing in our hands.

There is no map, no clue about where we came from or where we will go. But, hidden in the secret world of our DNA, are a few tools—the basic human traits. The urge to grasp is one of these. Our survival depends on it. It is in all of us to reach out and take hold, to bring things that lie beyond us to our mouths, our eyes and our hearts.

We begin taking hold with great enthusiasm as soon as possible; I have seen photos of babies in utero holding onto the umbilical cord. And once out, eager for life, we grasp whatever we can.

But the dying man's hands fall open. We leave as empty as we came.

It is said that Alexander the Great asked his statesmen to leave his arms dangling outside the coffin as they carried him through the streets for his funeral: "Let them all see that even I, world-conqueror, am leaving empty-handed."

In the end our hands are opened. We give life back. Empty we come. Empty we go. From emptiness to emptiness.

Some say that it is possible for emptiness to travel with us all the way through life. They say that to let it fill us is the greatest blessing and the greatest bliss. I have heard it said that Buddha asked that no statue be made of him after his death: "If you would like to remember me, keep an empty chair in the meditation hall. That would represent me better than any physical form."

When my meditation master Osho left his body, I wrote this haiku:

The elegant vase falls.

emptiness

everywhere.

An enlightened one seems to be emptiness itself. Osho was empty in every detail. His walk, his gestures, the silence between his words. And when he died, it spread out all over the place. The sky was empty. There was endless space in the peacock's eye. I even found the vacant center of my own heart.

Emptiness. Empty-ness: *First let me say something about* ness. *I think all the* ness *words are nests, the hollow that tenderly holds things, the cup-shaped space into which things are born, nurtured and set free. And so emptiness is the nest where empty grows.*

Now, Empty. *Empty tells a story with its sound: The* E *of empty is a soft, emotional utterance, a little cry of angst:* e–. *But it doesn't last long. Soon the lips are closed with the magical* M. *We bring in the contentment of* M, *as in mother, moon, memory (and macaroni!). We are hushed as the* mmm *vibrates in the skull and gently leads us to* p, *that soft sound of prayer and poetry, pleasure and promise. Our first syllable is complete: Our small cry of being lost in the night is met by the soothing presence of two of the most reassuring sounds made by the human voice:* e ... mmmppp ...

Now enter the tapping, sTriking *sound of* T. *Listen to how the* t *brings us into the here and now, how it awakens us.*

And the ee *sets us free. Assured and relaxed, yes. Allowed to sleep, no. We are awakened to the nothingness and urged to live it.*

I cleaned houses on and off, to fill in the economic gaps, for many years. I liked the work. It was absorbing, it was time alone with myself, and it was, by its very nature, transformative. I moved around a bit, going from sink to stove to refrigerator to floor ... and a miracle followed me: the room became new again.

The hidden reward in the work of cleaning is that something in the cleaner is also renewed in the process. Every cleaner talks about that moment when you turn for a last look at your freshly cleaned room, and sigh. Chaos has fled both inside and out. Simplicity and harmony prevail once more.

But I had to *learn* the joy of cleaning. Like most of us, I got the idea early in my childhood that cleaning was "dirty work" and best delegated, if at all possible, to someone else.

It seems my greatest teacher in the joy of cleaning was an unlikely lady with two-inch fingernails. Someone who looked like she had no idea what a scouring pad was. But once in a while, the compassion of life disguises herself as a character like this just to see if we're awake . . . and open.

This woman was brought into the restaurant where I was a cook to inspire us, the cooking staff, about the virtues of a clean kitchen. She was an administrator, with panty hose and high heels. She moved her smooth, perfectly manicured fingers as she spoke. They danced like ballerinas before us.

I looked down at my onion-stained hands with short, practical nails and possibly a bandage or two, and thought, Who does she think she is, anyway?

I was happy as a cook. The work was demanding and used so much of me. I was not even resentful when we stayed late, sometimes until three A.M. scrubbing down the grill and mopping the floor. But I was resentful of this uptown girl trying to tell us how to keep clean in the hot pot of a restaurant.

With my arms folded, standing sideways, giving her only one ear, I listened.

"There is only one secret to cleaning," she began. "You must approach it as creating beauty. Whatever it takes to make the space beautiful, do that.

"Whatever it takes. Sometimes you move things around, sometimes you take things away. You might add flowers, maybe you sweep the floor. But essentially, your motive is beauty."

When she left, my arms were still folded. I was still muttering to myself about her long fingernails, but I couldn't help trying to look at the kitchen the way she had described. And it turned out to be a wonderful game. I came into my eyes and learned how to please them. I found I could catch the morning light with a blue glass vase on the windowsill. I played at arranging the variously shaped spice bottles, the jars of grains and beans, the mixing bowls.

But what I came to see more and more was, almost always, subtraction created more beauty than addition. I learned that cleaning is a negative art. It is the art of erasing, of clearing away, of realizing what is essential, and giving it space.

My favorite story about emptiness is a small exchange between my five-year-old daughter and me. It is best told in the light of another life-changing moment; something that I experienced years before, which still gives my life direction, and which is described in loving detail in the chapter "R: Remembering."

We were celebrating the birthday of Julia's husband with dinner at a French restaurant. Julia, my best friend, called herself a "Christian Mystic." On the way to the restaurant, in the back seat of a VW van, in one of my life's most intimate conversations, I accidentally stumbled upon the great remembrance.

It was so difficult to describe what I experienced, even to myself, that I didn't attempt to tell anyone about it for weeks. But that night, when we returned from the restaurant to Julia's house, she sensed that something had opened in me. As soon as I had taken off my coat, she handed me a book.

The book was *Zen Flesh, Zen Bones,* a compilation of ancient Zen texts by Paul Reps. She opened to the Ten Ox-herding Pictures and had me turn the pages slowly. Each pen-and-ink picture was framed in a black circle. Together they seemed to tell a simple story: A young man appears, he sees the footprints of an animal, and follows them until he sees a bull. He catches the bull, tames it, and eventually rides it. But when one turns to the eighth picture, there is a surprise—the circle is empty.

The empty picture threw me into a silent gap. It seemed to perfectly describe what I had remembered that night. In the place I had touched upon, everything had disappeared: my search, the bull, the taming of the bull, the riding . . .

Grateful tears came to my eyes. So, I was not alone in this. There were at least a few people who had seen what I had seen, and who might be or might have been dedicated to returning to that place that the eighth ox-herding picture described so well.

I feel that we all have inklings about the emptiness inside us. When Dr. Deepak Chopra tells us that at the atomic level we are 99.9% space, we are relieved that, at last, the secret is out. In spite of appearances, we can feel our spaciousness.

My daughter, Sumanas, expressed such wonderings about inner space over breakfast one morning when she was five years old. Quite unusual for her, she ate in silence for a long time.

Then she looked up from her bowl of Cheerios and confessed, "You know, Mom, sometimes I think I'm Nothing just *dreaming* that I'm a person."

I stopped. All the thoughts in my mind, the plans for the day, the ongoing concerns about love or money, dissolved. Once again I was looking into that eighth ox-herding picture.

"Really?" I managed to say.

She went on, trying to describe this not-much-talked-about experience that she had stumbled upon. "Or sometimes it just feels like I'm the whole Earth, dreaming that I'm a person."

This time I fell through the gap in our conversation like Alice down the rabbit hole. I looked out at the child who was passing through my life and wondered who she was. I wondered who I, the falling one, was. I wondered about the feeling of being in a dream and who might be dreaming it.

So many years later, I still wonder at what this child was trying to tell me. The Nothing that was dreaming Sumanas seemed to be utterly full. It contained what the Taoists call "the ten thousand things": all the colors, smells and sounds, all the animals and plants and buildings and machines and toys and people, all the oceans and mountains, the sunshine and the rain: the whole world.

The Earth, it seems, lies in emptiness, full of nothing, and dreams of being a little girl eating a bowl of Cheerios . . . and a teenager trying to figure out the world. A little boy climbing a tree. And an old man dying. A woman writing a book. And somebody reading it.

And sometimes in the dream, the little girl or the teenager

or the little boy or the old man or the writer or the person looking into these pages, is given a glimpse of the whole, ridiculous, simple truth. Sometimes we wake up and feel like Nothing and the Whole Earth have come together and, just for the joy of it, are dreaming us up.

F: *Face*

ഒ൮൙ൕൖ

*All our lives we've looked
into each other's faces.
That was the case today too.
How do we keep our love-secret?
We speak from brow to brow
and hear with our eyes.*

—Rumi, *Birdsong*,
Versions by Coleman Barks

Face. A strange choice, perhaps, from the mysterious world of
Fears and Freedom; Forefathers, Farms and Feathers; Floating,
Flying and Flirting. But I have chosen "Face" because faces are
so much a part of everyday life and because, in moments when
we have the eyes to see, every face is a miracle.

If we really look into a face, we see a lifetime of stories pass
there. So much of a book is on its cover, if we open our eyes
and look. Sadly, we are taught not to look at faces—especially
the interesting ones. When we were children drinking up the
world with openmouthed abandon, a large, well-meaning person kept pulling us back. Until we learned the rules and closed
down the portholes, they kept whispering in our ears, "Don't
stare!"

This chapter is an invitation to once again drink up the world
around us. Especially the faces. Especially the interesting ones.

And so, Face. What song does this little word sing? F-ace.

F—a wonderful letter, a fun *sound, a* free *sound. Right from the
start, we show our two front teeth (bucked, crooked, straight, or
missing) and let it all hang out. Exposing ourselves to the world, all
our winds are allowed to blow: F-f-f-f.*

And now that we are out of hiding? A. *This is what is called the
long A. She is the strongest version of A. She is the sound of her
own name. She is not only saying, "Here I am." But, "I am what I*

am." And not only that, she is the first letter of the alphabet, sound coming into being, the awakening of our senses: A.

Now ce—*our jaw relaxes, our mouth softens;* ce *is an intimate whisper. Finishing* fa *with* ce *gives it grace. The* fa *in face tells us that here is one of us—unapologetic, unashamed. The* ce *in face asks that we use soft lighting when looking upon one another. Candlelight is good. Lovelight is best.*

This chapter has its stories, but it is more a meditation on the faces of our lives. Once in a group therapy session at the Osho ashram in India, we were asked to go, one by one, to the center of the circle and "be authentic." It seemed a nearly impossible but intriguing experiment. I decided to give it my all, not making any plans before it was my turn.

When at last I stood in the center of all of those people, the words that came out of my mouth were, "Who *are* you?!" I repeated this several times. The more I said it and looked around, the more authentic it became. I felt a certain panicked wonderment as I looked into the faces of a roomful of strangers—in the deepest meaning of the word.

The therapist came to me as I trembled with emotion in the middle of the room. "Good," he said and he led me to a mirror in the corner. "Now look into those eyes in the mirror and ask the same question."

"Who are you?" I asked, looking at my own face with at least as much awe and alarm.

"Good," he said again. Now he led me to a bigger-than-life picture on the wall of Osho, my beloved meditation master. "Now ask the same thing of this face."

I looked into those huge eyes and asked my question again, "Who *are* you?!"

Now I was totally bewildered. I had asked my question of everyone in the world: my master, myself and all the others. No answer seemed to be coming.

The therapist gently asked me one more question. "What is the difference, asking your questions in these three different places?"

"Not much," my answer came, surprising me with its truth.

"Not much," he repeated, helping me to hear my own words. "There is not much difference . . . ," he said again.

Looking back at him, I suddenly felt gratitude for the glimpse I had just been allowed into the mystery of us all. And gratitude to him as my guide—a perfect stranger.

A few weeks ago I went to the Sufi Dances in Ithaca, New York, which are held once a month. Usually more than one hundred people attend. We sing songs that are animated by arm movements, whirling and simple dance steps. The sound of our blended voices is deeply moving, but the most touching moments come during the "partner dances." In these dances, we turn to face a partner and sing a song of blessing to him or her, accompanied by heartful gestures.

As new people and new dances are added each month, there is a learning session before each song. Often, as we are learning the partner dance, singing to a person and looking into his/her eyes, the inevitable happens: We fall in love. And at that precise moment, the other inevitable happens: The winds of the dance change, and we are asked to turn and face a new partner.

Thus we make our way around the circle, falling in love again and again. Curtains removed from the eyes, we turn to the new face behind us and fall again. The experience is like moving through a montage of humanity: There are faces red and round, faces thin and pale. Wrinkled and old, young and shy, black and white, male and female.

And somewhere on our way around the circle, the magic happens. The differences we thought were so important for making our way in the world begin to fade. Even the categories of friend/foe/stranger lose their meaning. Each face is a door to something beyond us all.

In the Zen tradition there is a *koan* (a riddle used to focus one's meditation): "What face did you have before your mother was born?" The seeker is asked to meditate upon this riddle until the mind's answers fade away, and insight about one's true nature dawns.

When I was a cleaner in the commune, I came to fancy a clay figurine owned by one of the residents—a hooded, monklike character sitting with its knees drawn up and its head hung as if in contemplation. One day when I was dusting the shelf where the monk spent his days, I turned him upside down, curious to see his face.

I gasped. The hood was hollow. The whole sculpture was empty. I was looking into what is called in Zen "the original face." No face at all.

After a few rounds of a Sufi partner dance, I begin to see the face we all had before our mothers were born—the face as window looking into the place where love lives.

A last meditation on faces. This one is for, and about, my youngest daughter, Angelina, who, for delightful but complicated reasons, I call DP.

It turns out that DP and I were separated for most of the early years of her life. After the divorce, she went to live with her father in his new blended family, visiting me from time to time. Sumanas, her older sister, stayed mostly with me.

Because DP and I didn't spend days-in-and-out together, I couldn't take her face for granted. I saw that face, as it grew and changed, as I have never seen any other. When we were together, I bathed myself in her face.

When I think about my wonder over DP's face, I am reminded of my favorite scene in the play *Our Town*. After her untimely death, Emily is given the opportunity to relive one day of her life. What she sadly discovers is that no one takes the time to look at one another. "Oh, Mama, just look at me one minute as though you really see me . . . ," her ghost pleads while the mother scurries around trying to make a special birthday dinner for the daughter.

The mother cannot hear the ghost, and she takes the daughter's face for granted. Today is just too hectic. There will be another day to really look around and take it all in, she must have told herself.

But of course there never was. I am more fortunate . . . in a weird sort of way. I could not take DP's face for granted. I still can't.

When we were together, I would live with her on ground level, eye to eye. I would let in all the wonder pouring out of her. When we were apart, I would talk to her face in the picture on the mantel.

DP came to live with me many years ago. She is a teenager now and wonders why she can't seem to hide anything from me. I tell her I'm psychic, and since I've read palms for a living from time to time, she believes me.

But now you know my secret. And when you read this, DP, you will, too: I looked at you. I always look at you.

Here is a poem about your two-year-old face to prove it:

"*Angie-song*"

today your face
shone clear
through the crystal mountain air.
i saw you/oh
so clearly
in yellow overalls,
big curls catching sun,
bringing in the morning.

you're an inchworm child,
inching your curly body
deep inside of me.

i will keep you here
snug
in the kangaroo mama pouch
of my heart.

G: *God*

Love is wild.
Life is wild.
And God is absolutely wild.

—Osho, *Tantra:*
The Supreme Understanding

God.

(Oh God.) Am I really going to talk about God? To talk about God is always to enter a stormy sea. Still, once in a while, the ride's worth it. Grab a life jacket and hop in the boat!

The God I was introduced to in religion class was difficult for a child to love. He almost always seemed unkind and had no sense of humor. And once the Truth was discovered about Santa Claus and the Tooth Fairy, He wasn't believable, either. Being told in religion class that the greatest sin was to doubt Him only made matters worse: I disliked Him more, doubted Him more, and felt guiltier about all of it.

As a young girl in Catholic school, I managed to hide my aversion and mistrust, but battling my way through adolescence, I gathered the courage and steam to become a vociferous atheist: There was no God. We had created a big father figure to hide behind and I, for one, was not going to hide anymore!

On the other side of my teen rebellion, however, a little deeper into life, I began to wonder anew at the hugeness of it all.

Gradually a crack opened, allowing the possibility to enter me that there might be a great benevolence around (maybe even within) us. I decided to keep the book open.

I still sit happily in the world without conclusions. I try not to close the book about anything—especially not about God.

As we continually find ourselves in the middle of the story, how can we conclude anything just yet?

I guess I am a kind of agnostic-in-wonder-of-it-all. And here is a beautiful twist—the word agnostic comes from the Greek word *agnostos,* which not only means unknown, but unknowable.

English-speaking Jews write the name of God without a vowel: *G-D.* It is impossible to say it that way, and that's the idea. They took out the *O* so that when one comes across the word, he will be unable to say it and fall silent. That silence will convey what is trying to be said better than any word.

But for the sake of our sound game, we will use the version of God that can be spoken. Even though I don't know Him very well, I don't think He minds what we call Him. From my limited experience of His presence, He has more capacity for lightness than anyone I know.

So God: *g-od.* My father's last utterance was the sound of *g.* It was all he could get out. It was his last gift to us, his six children and wife, tearfully gathered around his hospital bed. He knew this was it, his last chance to say whatever was still unsaid. With great effort and assistance from my brothers, he rose up on his elbows and tried to speak.

"G . . . ," he began.

A deep listening silence descended on us all.

"G . . . ," he tried again, but had to stop for a breath.

"G . . . ,"—one more time. But the effort had exhausted him. He had swallowed too much air and now had the hiccups. A precious solitary tear dropped from his eye down his cheek, and we all heard what can never be spoken.

Later we would argue about what my father was trying to say with his "G. . . ." The irony was that everyone in my family had a name that started with *G,* including both of my parents! My mother was certain that he was trying to say "Gil," the name of my youngest brother, who was only nine when my father died. I was certain he was going to speak of something very profound, of goodness or grace or maybe even God, as his parting message to us all.

It was only years later that I felt I knew what he wanted to tell us in that last effort. My preschool-aged daughter heard me telling the story and enthusiastically added her opinion, "He wanted to say goodbye!"

Since that day, my daughter insists that she is the reincarnation of my father. Who knows? Maybe she is. But more important to me is that once again a child brought me back to Earth from the philosophical clouds of my mind. Surely my father wanted to wish us well in the simplest way possible. He wanted to tell us goodbye.

And so God lives with our goodbyes in the land of G. What else do we find there in that guttural sound? Grace *and* grateful. Gallant *and* grumpy. Guilt *and* grand. G. . . . *The lump in our throat is released. The fifth chakra, the energy center at the throat which is the center of truth-telling, is cleared. We are coming from our sense of what is true, in all its freshness as it is continually renewed.* G: *the Iron Curtain of our speech is lifted.*

od: *"awed." If we are going to fill in that space which the Jews keep between G and D, what better sound than "awe"? The state of openmouthed wonder. No thought can enter: awe.*

And we end with d, *that* Do *sound, that putting forth into creation.* G: *We are going to speak the truth,* O (awe): *but no words will say it,* D: *we offer our doing, we lend ourselves to the manifestation—* *"Thy will be done."* God.

Though I don't know much about Him, the one thing of which I'm certain is that God is nuts. If you look around, you'll see we're in the hands of a madman! Someone with great humor, exquisite taste and marvelous talent, but, without question, off the deep end.

Take this hypothesis with you on your next visit to the zoo. You'll find yourself wondering, "What mad genius designed these characters?" The monkey with the neon-colored face (some even painted at the other end), the flamingo's huge, hot-pink body balanced on one spaghetti-leg. The giraffe, the iguana, the anteater, the tree frog . . .

And another truth, deeper still, dawns on us at the zoo. When we look into the eyes of all those creatures, they look back. There is something of us in all of them; we are all made of the same stuff: consciousness.

The Hindus have an idea that God, Brahma, is putting on a play, a *Lila*, in which He takes on all the parts. The flamingos and the anteaters and the giraffes. The ostriches and the iguanas. The banyan trees sending down roots from their highest branches, the mushrooms that grow in the dark. He can be vicious like a tiger, generous like a dog, secretive as a frog who is shaped and colored exactly like a leaf. He has the grace of a swan, the clumsiness of a penguin on land, the flexibility of a willow tree. He plays the part of storms and rainbows, stars and people. Even you. Even me.

My favorite personal story about things that go on between God and His people is this one. It is from that meager corner of my life, which has generated so much wealth.

I had just returned from my first trip to India and I had not planned my finances very well. That is to say, I had not found a job yet, and my small savings were drying up very quickly, when I was stopped by a state trooper who told me that the inspection sticker on my truck had expired. (I had forgotten totally about the requirement for inspections.) He gave me a thirty-six-hour warning and sent me to the nearest inspection station.

As you might have guessed, the truck flunked on several counts. I needed one new tire and some bodywork, including mending a hole in the floor. Reluctantly, I used most of my remaining money to have the repairs done and then took the truck to another inspection station closer to home. This was a factory town in Maine with a lot of bricks, a lot of smoke, and a lot of poor people. The station attendant sadly told me I needed three more new tires to pass the inspection.

My heart broke and my eyes filled with tears, which I tried desperately to fight back. "I can't talk about this right now," I managed to say to him. "I need time to think about what to do. . . ."

And I ran across the street to a small stream on the other side. Somewhat hidden between its banks, I allowed myself to come undone. I wailed and cried and stomped and screamed.

I pulled up wild seedlings from the bank. I would have blown up the planet if I could. Things weren't fair. And I knew whose fault it was: God's!

"Where are you now, God?!" I cried to the sky. I had left everything and gone to India. I had worked hard, participated in growth groups where I tried to honestly look at my fears and greed. I had done all kinds of experiments in meditation to help dissolve the ego. . . . I had hoped for at least a little cooperation on the other end, a little help from my friend.

"Where are you now, God?!" I continued to yell through my stomping and tears.

And then I suddenly heard a gravelly voice calling to me, "Ma'am . . . ?"

It did not come from the sky. It came from a concrete bridge over the stream. It was not a divine voice, but one that came from a raspy, human throat.

"Ma'am . . . ?" he called again.

I looked up to find an old man in tattered clothes with barely any teeth. His face was stubbled with a few days' growth, and he wore a moth-eaten cap pulled down over his ears. He was a hobo, as my parents called such folks; a street-person as we might call him these days.

"Can I help you, ma'am?" he yelled with some difficulty through his scratchy throat.

In that moment, confronted by his genuine concern, the hardness in me melted. I looked at him and thought, "So this is where you are, God!" And my tears turned to laughter. Today at least, God seemed to have fewer resources than I did!

"No thanks!" I waved to him. The tension in my face and body must have visibly relaxed, because his did. "Thanks again," I called after him as he turned to leave.

If that's God, I thought affectionately as I watched him make his way down the street, I'd better find my own way out of this one. . . .

So I pulled myself together and walked up the bank. I had a checkbook and an empty account, which was more than God seemed to have at the moment. I had friends and a couple of brothers who might loan me money to cover the check until I could make ends meet. And somehow I knew I eventually would.

I walked across the street to the gas-station attendant who suddenly seemed to inhabit a much friendlier world. I told him to put on three new tires and wrote a "bad" check which I made "good" the next day.

And ever since that meeting, I walk through the world a little lighter, sensing that there might be something/someone out there who cares about me. He never pushes His way into my life, although once in a while, when I'm open to it, He sends me a message. Mostly He just watches. He has more faith in me than I do.

H: *Hands*

꒰꒱꒱

In the morning sow thy seed,
and in the evening withhold not thine hand.

—Ecclesiastes, 11:6

Hands.

I open my palmistry workshops by having students write about loved ones' hands. This is before I present anything about the art and science of palmistry, and everyone is amazed to discover so many detailed memories and such a wealth of feeling about hands: how unique each person's are, how much they say to us.

When participants read the pieces they have written on the hands they know and love, the room grows quiet. Often, at least once in the go-around, there are tears. We enter a surprisingly delicate matter when we think about the hands that have helped to carry us through life. Hands are, after all, those extremities of our bodies with which we reach out and touch.

Hands. What poetry is in the sound of this word: hands. Hands are rightly blessed to begin with H, the alphabet's sigh. Hands are in the family of hearts and homes, healing, hearth, and happiness. Yes, the family's dark side includes horror, hate and hell, but one cannot blame H for what these words have become. H as a beginning brings warmth.

Ayurvedic *health practitioners prescribe making the sound of H for chronic stomach disorders. Try it. It's a lot like laughing. And so we begin our message about hands with a lightness and warmth that let our bellies relax: h . . .*

Now Aaannn. *The* a *is feminine. It is the soft sound of the letter* A. *So we relax with* h, *become receptive with* a, *and enter the meditative chamber of* n. *If you close your eyes and hum a prolonged* n, *you will feel why this is the sound which* ayurvedic *doctors prescribe for ear infections. It pushes back the bombardment of sounds from the outer world and bathes the ears in a soothing vibration.*

Relaxed, receptive, alone with ourselves, we enter the strong, clear, masculine sound of d—*the Doer, the creator, the bringer into being:* hand.

One of my earliest memories is of looking at my own hands. Perhaps every child passes through this moment as he grows into his own. I was awake on my bed, alone in the dark, when I began to wonder at the experience of being alive. I found myself suddenly surprised that I inhabited a body, and that it was at my command. With deep interest, I performed simple experiments. I decided to lift my arm and then watched it rise into the space around me. I wiggled my fingers and watched as they danced for me in the moonlight.

It felt like an incredible secret that I was hidden so perfectly inside this strange mechanism. I felt that no one suspected, not even my parents, that it was me who actually lived in here!

How mysterious. What a precious discovery. In my heart of hearts, I had found a place that was all my own.

My father fell into a peculiar fascination with his hands when the brain tumor moved his mind from the terrain of logic to less solid ground. He seemed to be having an intense dialogue with his hands. He would hold them up at chest level with one palm facing the ceiling, the other facing the floor. At regular intervals, the hands would reverse positions—upturned hand facing the floor, downturned hand facing the ceiling—at which point, my father would stare at them, dumbfounded.

It was a great puzzle to all of us who spent time with him while he was in the hospital undergoing radiation treatments. But it was my good fortune that one day he revealed his secret to me. In that exchange at his bedside, my father passed on the torch of his life's quest. This is my true inheritance.

As always, Providence made impeccable arrangements for

this torch-passing ceremony. The funding for my job at the university counseling center mysteriously disappeared in the exact week that my father was diagnosed with a brain tumor. I was laid off and consequently free to travel to upstate New York to be with him.

He was in the hospital when I arrived, and I went with my mother that afternoon to visit him. He seemed happy to see me, but not as surprised as I would have thought. He looked at me through eyes that had less of the Dad-I-knew in them. They seemed to tunnel back into a curious new place inside. Or maybe it was an old place. Very old and very familiar, at least to him.

After a short visit with my father, I went into the hall with my mother, who was fighting back tears and shaking with emotion. She took out a cigarette, and I asked her for one. I had not smoked for years, but I shared one with her now.

"Has anyone told him what's going on? About the tumor?" I asked behind the comfort of our cigarettes.

"No," my mother replied, still shaking. "I haven't had the courage. . . ."

"We need to tell him," I said.

She nodded.

"Maybe we can do it together," I offered.

My mother seemed pleased, and we put out our cigarettes and went back into the room to tell him.

"Do you know what's happening to you?" I asked him. "Why you're in the hospital?"

"No," he said, his eyes revealing a pure state of not-knowing.

"You have a tumor," my mother said. "In the head." She motioned around her own head.

"Really?" he responded as though he had been told an amazing scientific fact about something on the other side of the world.

Later we found out that the doctors had told him more than once already. We were to tell him a few more times, as well. Each time he responded as though he were receiving a very interesting fact about life on a distant planet.

For the two weeks that I visited my father in the hospital, sitting at his bedside became my meditation. I would often spend ten hours a day with him, and instead of trying to interest him in my world, I tried to enter his.

It was a fascinating world. Huge pieces of his life were apparently missing from his memory, but his childhood was there in meticulous detail. And he was more free than I ever remembered him. He talked about feelings that he had never dared to share with me. He spoke easily about personal doubts regarding religion and relationships and the roles we take on but don't really believe in.

We did not converse all the time. There were long periods of silence when he would eat his lunch, or when the two of us would just look out the window into that other world where everyone still moved with such conviction and at such a hurried pace.

We enjoyed several games together. My favorite involved making scribbles for each other. We were to make something of the other's scribble by adding lines and shadings. From my father's scribbles, I remember making teacups, plates with food on them, animals and people's faces. From my scribbles, my father made intricate designs. The man who had always scoffed at modern art would turn the paper around and around admiring his abstract doodles. Sometimes he would look up at me with excitement in his eyes. "How 'bout that?!" he would exclaim. "Pretty good, don't you think?"

Eventually my father began to speak to me about the game with his hands. It seems it was a symbolic play, a dramatization. It allowed him to explore a profound lesson that his life was showing him.

He would put his hands out in front of him, one palm down, one palm up. Then he would begin the drama. "My whole life . . . ," he would say as he began to make visible efforts to turn the upturned hand down. "I'd try and I'd try and I'd try . . ." At this point he would exaggerate the effort to the point where the upturned hand would shake. It was as if he was trying to turn over a huge stone.

At some point, with immense effort, he would succeed in turning the hand over, palm down. But at that very moment, the other hand would suddenly turn up, so he was left again with the same pattern in reverse.

He looked at me with raised eyebrows and continued, "And then again I try and try and try . . ." Now the newly upturned hand would show tremendous effort to turn itself over. And, as you might have guessed, as soon as my father succeeded in this difficult task, the downturned palm popped up again. He looked at me now with even wider-eyed bewilderment.

The demonstration was over at this point. But often in our silent moments, I would turn from gazing out the window and find his attention intently on his hands, slowly turning one over—only to find the other popping up.

After my father performed this drama for my mother, she would try in every way to have the hands come out right. I remember her once trying to physically stop the hand about to turn over. "See?" she would say. "They're together."

In the face of losing her lifetime friend, my mother was desperately seeking a way out of the helplessness she felt. But my father looked at her sadly when she did this. At that point, she was unable to embrace the understanding he had come upon. He had stumbled onto the Stuff of Life and was reveling in the wonder of it.

He had found the secret that could—and eventually would—release him from his endless struggle: that which cannot be changed; the balance which, despite our efforts, always re-creates itself. In the world of Zen, this is called "Suchness." My father renamed it in sign language: one palm up, one palm down.

I: *Innocence*

❦

*Unless you become as little children, you
cannot enter the kingdom of heaven.*

—Matthew, 18:3

Perhaps you remember Antoine de Saint-Exupery's test for innocence in *The Little Prince*. He would show the person in question a drawing he had made, as a six-year-old, of a boa constrictor who had just eaten an elephant. If the person took it for a hat, as unfortunately all "grown-ups" seemed to do, he would know "not to talk to that person about boa constrictors, or primeval forests, or stars . . .

"I would bring myself down to his level. I would talk to him about bridge, and golf, and politics, and neckties. And the grown-up would be greatly pleased to have met such a sensible man."

I read *The Little Prince* often, and whenever I do, I try to look at that drawing as though I have never seen it before. Eventually I see the little eye in the rounded brim of the "hat," but I know in my heart that I have been indoctrinated well enough to pass for a "grown-up." My child-eyes are weak. Even so, once in a blessed while, the magic does reach me.

What does the sound of Innocence tell us? I: i is the highest vowel sound. Both forms of the letter I bring our voices up into the head, into the space between the eyes, into the "third eye [I!]." The long form of I (as in me, myself and) stands strong. It is a statement: I. But the softer i of innocence is not so sure of anything. It is an open, tentative sound. A good beginning to innocence.

NN . . . *We have two of them. We are asked to dwell for an extra beat in the sound of* nn *before going anywhere. One* n, *vibrating in the ears, shutting out the external world of sound, brings us home. Two* nn's *make sure we are alone with ourselves.*

And now o, *the round, deep sound which looks just like it sounds. I have recently heard of experiments where a plate of sand is placed on a speaker through which the vowel sounds are played. The researchers claim that pictures of the letters are created in the sand by the vibration of their sounds. In order to really believe this experiment, I would need to see the plates of sand for all the vowels—except* O. *Intuitively, it just feels right. Don't we feel the shape of* O *whenever we sing her song? Round, whole, empty at the center:* O.

So first we come into our third [I] eye, the chakra—or energy center in the body—that is the seat of unmotivated vision. When we are centered in the third eye, we see things as they are, not as we hope or fear they might be. From this place of pure seeing, we enter a private space with the lingering sound of a double n, *leading us to discover the inner* o, *round, whole and deep.*

Now cence. *This is exactly the sound of the word "sense," which means to feel. It indicates that we are to experience life directly. Listen to the sound of "cence/sense":* c(s) *is the Softest sound in the English language, followed by the short sound of* e, *a little cry of angst—the sound of vulnerability. We end with* nce *which reassures us that we can stay alone and soft on this journey home: innocence.*

As I sit at my computer writing this, I have been looking at a photo of my children when they were six and nine. They are standing in the California sunlight, pink-cheeked and relaxed. How unself-conscious they look beneath gigantic hats made of painted foam—one hat in the shape of a dolphin, the other a monkey. They have not yet figured out that inside that little black box, a record of the moment is being made. They are not thinking that one day a photo will appear, which people will look at and make comments about. All that is too far away.

It was my great (and terribly naive) hope to keep this spirit alive in my children forever. I hoped they would never have to fall. That they would never be tempted to taste the fruit of knowledge of good and evil. That they would never come to see themselves as anything less than perfect and whole.

But slowly the smoky veil of sophistication descended over them. They joined me in the grown-up boat, where we are all lost at sea.

Sometimes the dove with an olive branch in her beak flies over us—the motley crew in this boat—and we feel the promise of another shore: the Land of Second Innocence. A land occupied by sages—elders with eyes of children.

The Second Innocent is a rare flower. He knows the whole story. He knows old age, sickness and death. He knows violence, betrayal and loss. And still he is here without argument, bathing himself in whatever is.

Have you ever known an old person with the straightforward wisdom of a child? His innocence is the most brilliant. He is good-humored in the face of corruption; he knows it isn't serious; he has made the round-trip.

Here is my favorite story about innocence. It is the story of bringing a young boy to a nude beach.

When my daughter Sumanas was a preteen, she heard about Black's Beach, San Diego's well-protected nude beach, accessible only by a mile-or-so walk along the shoreline or by climbing up and down some steep cliffs.

She and a few of her friends were bubbling to see people actually walking around without clothes and acting as though nothing special were happening. I felt that a trip there would be therapeutically educational—to glimpse the possibility that one does not need to be ashamed of the body, and that nudity does not have to mean sex.

After rounding up Sumanas's friends, we went to her father's house to pick up her younger sister, DP. When their five-year-old half brother begged to come along, I agreed to take him, causing big frowns of disappointment in the room. Surely this meant that we'd have to go somewhere more civilized. Ray's mother was more conservative than I, and she would probably think of this outing as neither educational nor therapeutic.

Once in the car, however, we devised a plan. It was still early in the day, a cool one at that; the beach would not be very crowded. I would take Ray to some empty corner of the beach and divert his attention away from any nudity he might report back to his mother.

The plan went surprisingly well. We made it down the steep, narrow trail without seeing anyone unclothed. The beach was relatively empty but for a group of nude bathers at one end. The other end was totally empty.

I left the girls on a sand mound, where they tried to decide if anyone dare take off a particle of clothing. Then Ray and I walked a short distance down the beach to make a sand castle.

All went well as I situated myself so I could see the girls and other bathers, while Ray faced endless, empty beach. We dug and built and chatted until I saw Trouble coming our way: A fully naked man in sneakers carrying a boogie board.

"A sand castle, huh?" I heard him say, as he came within a foot of us and stopped.

Already surprised that we were not alone, Ray turned to face a greater surprise. There in broad daylight, at exactly Ray's eye level, hung the most exposed private parts that he had ever seen.

I had a brief conversation with the admirer of our castle; Ray said nothing. He sat there with his mouth wide open, occasionally nodding to a question or comment made by the surfer.

Our visitor eventually went on his way, and we resumed the building of the castle. We adorned our creation with stones and shells, and made a flag of seaweed on a stick. Then we decided to go back and join the girls.

As we were walking together down the beach, Ray finally broke his silence.

"You know, there's one thing I can't figure out," he said, carrying his pail and shovel and looking straight ahead.

"What's that?" I asked, curious as to what might be going on in that virgin mind.

Now he looked up at me and posed the big question: "How did that guy remember his sneakers and forget his bathing suit?"

J: *Joke*

*Then I commended mirth, because a man
hath no better thing under the sun, than
to eat, and to drink, and to be merry.*

—Ecclesiastes, viii

A taxi driver and a preacher from the same neighborhood in lower Manhattan find themselves together at the Pearly Gates. Saint Peter welcomes the taxi driver with a warm hug and tells him that his wings, halo, cloud and harp are waiting for him inside. The taxi driver thanks Saint Peter and runs through the gates.

The preacher piously walks up to Saint Peter's desk, ready to be given his reward for a life lived in celibacy, poverty and charitable works. Saint Peter looks at him sympathetically and says, "I'm sorry, you have been assigned to the Other Place."

The preacher is incensed. "How can this be?" he protests to Saint Peter. "I know that man you just welcomed into heaven. He is a gambler, a drunk and a womanizer. He uses foul language in every sentence!"

"I'm sorry," says Saint Peter, "I just follow the rules."

"What kind of rules does Heaven have these days to let in a taxi driver who committed sins every waking hour and to refuse a preacher?" asks the indignant man of the cloth. "I have been serving Our Lord. I do selfless work and preach His gospel every day!"

"That's just the problem," Saint Peter tells the minister. "When you preached, everybody fell asleep. But when that man took his customers for a ride in his taxi, they not only stayed awake. They prayed!"

Joke. Let's see what this little gem brings to our ears. We start with a joyful sound, a jewel of a sound: j. Just try it. The tongue is loose in the mouth; the teeth sit lightly together in front (a lot like those tissue and comb harmonicas we made in grade school); and we send a vibration up out of the throat: It's a Jug band sound. Raw, unsophisticated music.

Now o. O is Mother Nature's favorite form. It seems to be what comes easiest for her: rain falling on a lake, the age rings of an old tree, the center of so many flowers. The planet itself is a huge O.

Rounding our mouths and making the sound of o connects us to our world. We are no more separate, isolated egos; we have joined the circle of life. Letting it come from deep in our belly, feel the joy in it: o!

K: here's where the surprise comes in. We came out to play with J. We sounded the joy of connecting with O. And now comes that striking sound of k. Out from the land of karate and kisses and koans, it jumps us. It is quick. It is direkt. We are jolted out of our wits; it is a case of kiss and run.

Some of my favorite jokes are about religion. Other good ones are about sex, cultural/racial differences, politics—Serious Subjects. This is their magnetism. Waltzing us right into the forbidden zone, they get us to hold our breath and listen up.

The joke begins with a plausible situation, something we can relate to. But at a certain point, the story takes an unexpected turn and we find ourselves upside down. Our pockets are emptied of our heaviest secrets. Thus en*light*ened, we laugh.

I am always happy to take a sojourn to the planet of laughter. Though I am still vulnerable to the sticky web of Serious Subjects, I hope that life will tickle me out of any blinders that keep me from seeing the beauty of a good joke. What I mean is, I hope to be able to take life, in all her forms, lightly.

Even death—the Great Granddaddy of Serious Subjects. At least by the time I meet that angel, I hope I will have cleared my decks of valuable concerns so I can fly off with him. A little foreshadow came over me once, suggesting that this may actually be possible.

Once during a guided visualization in a workshop I was attending, I had the opportunity to meet an eccentric and cheerfully detached old woman, someone who, to this day, I can't seem to get out of my heart. The facilitator had taken us through the primeval forests of our minds to a beach. She told us that we might see a person sitting there. Sure enough, a white-haired old lady in a long robe was sitting alone on my beach. I walked up to her timidly, feeling awkward to be approaching a stranger.

As I stood at her side, she did not look up at me, but continued to stare straight ahead into the blue horizon. At last, trying to appear casual, I stuffed my hands into the pockets of my cutoff jeans and remarked, "Pretty day, isn't it?"

She still did not turn to face me, but smiled slightly and nodded.

"I was drawn to come over and talk to you," I tried to explain my unusual forwardness. "You seem familiar. Actually, I think you remind me of *myself* somehow. . . ."

Now she turned to me with penetrating eyes and said, "Why, I *am* you, dear."

At which point, my heart skipped a beat. I looked at her. Even though something about her had reminded me of myself, I didn't think she looked *that* much like me. For one thing, she was *old*.

"Let's see," she continued to look into me with ocean-deep eyes. "Where are you now in your life?" She did not wait for my answer: "Oh, yes, your father is dying. . . . This is an important passage; you will learn a lot of things from spending time with death. Things that will surprise you. For one, you are going to learn how to laugh."

Though the thought of it seemed strange, I did sense that laughter might be something death could teach, maybe the thing death teaches best. After all, my father had already confessed to me that, in the face of his own mortality, his mountain of worries had been reduced to an anthill. "Nothing was worth the worry I put into it," he had said. And since his graceful departure, not only has death ceased to be the dreadful monster I once imagined, but it has become the subject of many of my favorite jokes. For example:

A doctor telephones one of his patients who has just been subjected to a battery of medical tests. "I have some bad news and some worse news," the doctor begins. "Which would you like first?"

"Well, I'd like to go slowly with this," the stunned man on the other end of the line responds. "Let's start with the bad news first."

"OK," says the doctor. "You have only twenty-four hours to live."

"That's the *bad* news?! Whatever could be worse than that?!" exclaims the patient.

The doctor replies, "I've been trying to get you since yesterday."

My old-lady self and my dying father gave me my first adult flying lessons in humor, but the wisdom of a child secured the roots of my laughter in the mud of day-to-day life. In a short conversation with my five-year-old daughter, I learned the secret to that delightful, ever-ready childhood guffaw that all parents and other guardians of little people know and love. I was given a brilliant approach to life's most bewildering passages, a technique that involves watching for certain signs—like disappointment or anger—and reading them like cue cards held high from the back row [TIME TO LAUGH]:

My daughter Sumanas was in kindergarten and had just learned about the world of jokes. Most of what she found funny were "knock, knock" jokes and riddles about Moby Pickle ("What's big and green and lives under the sea?")—those jokes that grown-ups tolerate because it's such fun to watch children enjoying themselves.

Sumanas had become so enchanted with joking that she was beginning to make up her own jokes, most of which had a basic element missing. The most important element of all jokes, of course, is the surprise ending, and Sumanas's jokes were not lacking in surprise. They were, however, skimpy on the other end: logic. Just stories with no plotline at all, or strange riddles followed by unrelated strange answers.

One morning when Sumanas was trying a batch of home-made jokes on me, she came to one that was so obscure I had to tell her, "I don't get it."

She looked at me dumbfounded for a moment and then explained, "You're not *supposed* to get it! It's a joke!"

Her reprimand nudged a small laugh from me. "What do you mean that I'm not supposed to get it?" I asked.

"That's how you know it's a joke," she told me, with some exasperation that this must be explained. "Someone says something and you don't get it. Then you think, 'It must be a joke; I guess I'll laugh!' "

As much as I can remember, I try to return to Sumanas's ridiculously wonderful point of view. When I don't get it, I look around for the cue card and it's almost always there: "MUST BE A JOKE!" The cardholder himself shrugs as he raises his sign. Guess I'll laugh.

K: *Kisses*

I would love to kiss you.
The price of kissing is your life.

Now my loving is running toward my life shouting,
What a bargain, let's buy it.

—Rumi, *Open Secret*

Kiss!

Let's jump right into its sound: "Kiss!" It's a sassy word, quick and crisp. It does not meander; it comes right through the lips and plants itself somewhere. There is no mistaking it. When you're kissed, you always know it.

Opening with K is a strong beginning. Although the letter C can make this sound, she also has the flexibility to go soft, as in circle and cinema, or to go warm, as in chuckle and chum. K is not such a chameleon. He is consistently strong—and strange.

K is a strange fellow, a foreigner. He is perhaps the most exotic letter in the English language. So many of our K words are imported from remote lands: kabbalah, koala, kayak, kiwi, karate, karma.

K is also strong. Hearing the sound of this letter, we are made alert. Something's on its way. It may be kind *or it may* kill. *We sit up and pay attention.*

Now issss. Feel the short i sound vibrating in the center of your forehead, bringing you into the "third eye," into the psychic eye from which you see clearly, from which you can see the inner world where love is King.

Awake and watchful, we feel the possibility of love and melt: ss. Not briefly as with one s; we linger. Soft and softer still. Kiss.

Let me start my kiss story with a confession: I'm cheating on this one. The story will be more about Doris than kissing.

But I used up *D* with Dance, and the thing about Doris was that, above all else, she was an irrepressible kisser. The telling of this story is my kiss to her.

I first met Doris at a mountaintop gathering in honor of Ram Dass, ex-Harvard psychology professor turned entertaining translator of Eastern Mysticism—folk hero to us war-boom babies. I had seen flyers around town announcing that anyone interested in meeting Ram Dass could come to a certain house in the White Mountains on Sunday. "Bring food," the flyer said.

It was an hour's drive from the hills of Gorham, Maine, into the mountains. There were four of us in the car, all very excited to meet a modern-day "holy man" face-to-face.

We were among the first to arrive, and as we pulled into the nearly empty parking area, we wondered if we were in the wrong place. But as soon as we stepped out of the car, a group of people came running down the mountain, waving their arms and shouting hellos: odd-shaped folks, people with strange faces and very round heads.

I remember standing there with my mouth open as this entourage cheerfully descended the hill. "What is this?" I said to myself. "The spiritual seekers of today certainly come in strange packages."

One bearded, elflike creature ran directly for me, hugging me with all his might. Then he took hold of my shoulders and drew back, looking deep into my eyes. "It's been such a *long* time," he said.

I looked back at him, feeling an eerie sense of familiarity. Eerie because I was sure we'd never met (in this lifetime anyway). "It sure has!" I assured him.

The strange people led us up the hill where someone of normal proportion appeared, telling us with a friendly smile that we had arrived at Greenhill Farm and, yes, Ram Dass had already arrived. And isn't the view of the White Mountains spectacular? And isn't this a wonderful place for these folks to live together instead of in the institutions for retarded folks in town?

So that was it, my friends and I smiled at one another. Soon we found our way onto a large expanse of lawn where the festivities were to take place. Ram Dass was standing at one end, leaning on a walking stick, talking with two or three eager-looking people. Seeing him so accessible, I suddenly felt shy. I did not know how to approach someone who was both famous and holy—someone I'd always seen as a faraway figure on a stage. I looked for other things to do.

There were some Greenhill residents setting things up under a tent to serve lemonade. One of them was Doris, a tallish woman with short-cropped, dirty-blond hair, her jaw frozen in a pronounced underbite. She wore extremely colorful clothing, nothing matching anything else in texture, season, color scheme or era. I noticed that she had a certain awareness of her surroundings beyond that of her peers. She walked up to me without hesitation. "And how are you, Sister?" she asked.

"Great," I chirped, happy to move out of my self-consciousness. "And how are you?"

"Fine," she answered, edging closer. And then she took hold of the necklace I was wearing—a traditional Indian *mala*, a symbol of spiritual initiation strung with sandalwood beads and bearing a locket carved into the shape of "Om" (the symbol for the "eternal sound"). I had received this *mala* from my yoga teacher.

"Nice beads," Doris said, her lower jaw protruding more than ever.

"They are, aren't they?" I replied, beaming, my spiritual ego raising its head. A real live Indian Guru had put these *mala* beads over my head. This artifact made me one of the "in" crowd. Especially on a day like today.

As I was admiring my laurels and their obvious worth (even this retarded woman had seen the specialness), Doris blurted out, "Can I have 'em?"

This set me back on my heels. "Well, I don't think so," I responded, clutching the *mala* to my chest. "They are really very special beads.... They were given to me by a yogi...."

"That figures," Doris said flatly, and she turned away.

This was not the last time that Doris stopped me in my unconscious tracks and made me see my own self-deceptions. And though I didn't yet know that she would eventually be held in my memory as one of my clearest teachers, I had my first clue that something could be learned here!

In time, things arranged themselves so that I was on staff at Greenhill Farm, and Doris was an intimate character of my day-to-day landscape. Because my previous specialty as a counseling psychologist had been groups, I was given the role of leading group therapy sessions at Greenhill Farm.

I announced to the residents that we would be meeting every Thursday afternoon when everyone returned from the sheltered workshop. All seemed generally pleased that "something" was going to happen. They liked scheduled events, which usually involved such things as bowling, roller skating, picnics or movies.

When Thursday afternoon arrived, I ushered the group into the living room and asked them all to sit down. Arnold, a charming man in his forties who spent most of his time drawing trucks with Magic Markers, sat on the piano stool. Tommy, a twenty-year-old man with Down's syndrome, sat on the floor as he always did, his back against the couch, his head drooping. The others took seats, each assuming his or her own unique posture for waiting: Jim sat at the edge of the group on a dining-room chair, looking over his right shoulder again and again; Rosalie gazed off into space while kicking the base of her chair; the fingers of Sara's left hand played on the neck of an imaginary fiddle while she rocked in time and stroked her leg with the other hand; Doris sat next to me in an overstuffed chair, her legs crossed and her arms folded over her chest, grinning.

When all were settled, I cleared my throat and made my usual group-opening remark, "We are going to meet every week so we can talk to one another."

The members of the group looked at me blankly.

"We are going to talk about our *feelings*," I added, hoping to get right to the point.

Nothing registered on anyone's face. Though Doris's top leg started kicking, she kept on grinning.

"Let's start with you, Doris," I began. Doris was my brightest hope.

Unflinching, she looked right at me.

"Doris, I'd like you to tell Arnold how you feel about him," I instructed. I'd had a lot of experience with this one. It was a tried-and-true pump-primer.

"I love 'im," Doris said, unfolding and then refolding her arms over her chest.

Arnold, a devoted rocker by nature, rocked back and forth on the piano stool. "Thank you, Doris, thank you, thank you," he said, never lifting his head.

Beautiful! I thought. Things are moving right along. "Doris, can you say that directly to Arnold?" I prompted.

"I love you, Arnold," she said in the same simple tone.

"Thank you, Doris, thank you, thank you." Arnold continued rocking.

"Good," I praised (now let's see if we can thicken this plot). "Doris, can you tell Arnold *why* you love him? What are some things that make you love Arnold?"

Now there was an awkward pause as Doris looked helplessly at me. She unfolded and refolded her arms again, and finally said, "I just love 'im," after which she moved her jaw forward and gave me her biggest grin.

"Thank you, Doris, thank you, thank you. . . ."

That was the first, and last, group therapy session that I "facilitated" at Greenhill Farm. After that, we did yoga on Thursday afternoons.

Doris had managed to leave me with my ridiculous psychologist's question in my lap, and an emptier mind where the mystery of love found room to spread its wings again.

I have never asked that question of anyone since that day: "Why do you love _____?" Not even about me. I don't even like the poem that states: "Let me count the ways . . ." A sure sign that love is blowing through me is losing count. And the most certain thing we know about the flutter of love, is that it is not in our hands.

K: Kisses. We're closer than you think.

Doris had several delightful habits. One was that she called everyone—friend, foe and stranger alike—"Sister" or "Brother." Another was that, while she mostly remained aloof with someone she disliked, Doris was very free in demonstrating affection.

This included kissing. Not just with intimate friends, but

with perfect strangers. If the vibration was right, of course. Doris would walk into a restaurant, for example, and immediately case the joint. If she was moved by anyone there, and she usually was, she would walk up to her/him with a warm "Hello, Sister (Brother)!" and deliver a nice juicy kiss.

One afternoon I was approached by one of the Greenhill Farm staff and told that we were beginning a behavior-modification program to stop Doris from kissing.

"Good heavens, why?" I asked.

"Because it isn't *appropriate!*" The staff member looked at me as though I'd just been beamed down from Mars. She must have seen in my eyes that she still hadn't connected to the reasonable part of my brain. She honestly looked like she was trying hard to keep a grip on her patience, which was getting lathered up like a bar of soap, ready to jump out of her hands. "You can't just go around kissing people—in public places!"

I refused to participate in any behavior-modification program to stop Doris from kissing. At first I went gallantly into battle against the windmills of "social progress" for the developmentally disabled, but this was, in fact, the beginning of the end for me at Greenhill Farm. As time wore on, more and more of my conversations with staff members ended with my staring blankly at them.

I guess a little of Doris had rubbed off on me. From all my friends at Greenhill I had learned one important thing about political struggles: They aren't worth having.

Before leaving my special mountaintop school, I received a few spontaneous How-are-you-today-Sister? kisses from Doris. And I always felt blessed by them. I trusted Doris because she never doubted her own sense of things ... and she always sealed it with a kiss.

L: Let-Go

~~~~~~

*Think to yourself
that every day is your last;
the hour to which
you do not look forward
will come as a welcome surprise.*

—Horace

It's probably no accident that I'm beginning a chapter on let-go with my arm in a sling.

This is not the story I planned to write here. When I organized my life's miracles into a recipe for alphabet soup, this miracle was still in my blind spot. But by virtue of the universe's exquisite timing, I have been thrown into a fresh experience of let-go. The ground has been tilled, and I am invited to dig in.

"Let-go." What secrets might we find in its sound?

We open with L, the light, lilting, lyrical sound. The tongue turns up and gives birth to laughter, love, light. Let-go begins with levitation. We stop holding onto the rope, but we don't fall.

Now we make the short e sound of E. It sounds like the beginning of a cry: e. It expresses a feeling of smallness, powerlessness. But in comes our wake-up call: the sharp tap of T! Suspended in the air with L, we cry at our helplessness with e, and get hit with a sTick: T!

It seems so unfair, being hit when we are at our most vulnerable. Insult added to injury, we utter g, the sound that speaks of struGGle. The letter G is our most effortful sound: grunt, groan and grasp. The entire sound is made in the throat, where our fifth-energy wheel spins. There are seven such wheels—chakras in Sanskrit—whirling along our spine, each with its own psychic focus. The fifth chakra, at the throat, is the center of truth. Perhaps the g we make there indicates that we are enGaged in mustering the courage to speak truth. G—

we have started the engine that might propel us beyond the lies we
live with, especially those we tell ourselves.

Ironically, we are at the polar opposite of let-go now: We are
anxious, hit and struggling. But isn't this exactly how let-go happens?
For a few days after I gave birth to DP, I occupied a room right next
to the labor room. I remember hearing the labors escalate, the women's
voices becoming increasingly louder. And I noticed that every woman
eventually came to shouting, with great urgency: ''I can't take it
anymore!'' At which point there was the shuffling of many slippered
feet, as the labor bed was wheeled into delivery. A few minutes later,
nurses were running excitedly down the hall announcing that it was
a boy or girl, how many pounds, and so on.

I have watched it in my own life. At the exact moment when I
can't take it anymore, something major shifts. It feels like I'm losing
something I have been trying hard not to lose. But look what comes
of it: fresh life. Birth.

And so, at the peak of our hanging-on, comes O—the great healer,
the return to wholeness. O-O-O . . . We Open. We let the wind take
us. Maybe we even let ourselves fall, but, by way of the universe's
endless compassion, we seem to always land on soft ground.

A few weeks ago I was in a hurry. The hurry didn't come
all at once, I had to build up to it. I had responded to certain
details of my life by becoming increasingly frantic.

Over the last months I had started to feel old. Old. I was
approaching fifty and I had not gotten my life together yet!
Time was running out on the meter and I was still waiting in
line.

You know what happens when your car is out of gas, you're
already late for your appointment, and you're in the grocery
line that never moves. Your mind itches. You start calculating
everything, both past and future: how you could have avoided
the situation, theories about how to choose the quickest grocery
line, which exit you'll take on the way out, where you'll stop
for gas, what excuse you'll give when you finally arrive at your
destination.

This is how it was with me when I started out for a trip to
the Catskill Mountains in New York two Sundays ago: itchy
brain. I was not late for my particular appointment, I was late

for my life. I was calculating hard: what wrong turns I might have taken on the Road of Life; in what ways my children must have suffered because of my "open-ended" ways; what options were still open. Interwoven with the profound questions were an equal number of mundane concerns: where I'll stop for a rest this afternoon, what book I'll read tonight. Should I apply for that part-time job? Where will I get lunch on the way home tomorrow . . . ?

Just outside of town, I pulled up to the stop sign and found my view was blocked by a parked U-Haul truck. I pulled backward to adjust my view and saw a small patch of road from which I tried to calculate the traffic flow. When things looked clear, I pulled out, only to find a car rocketing toward me from behind the blind spot the truck had created.

Attempts to avoid the other car failed. There was the squealing of brakes, a loud crash, and my calculations stopped. It was clear that nothing was in my hands anymore; watching took over.

By the time the car had come to a stop, shreds of paint all over my dress, warm liquid running down my neck, people running in the road toward me, most of the fear I usually carry around had left me. The worst had happened, so what to fear?

Everybody told me not to move, and I was grateful. This was easy. I wasn't going anywhere. Surrounded by police, firemen and medics, I gave up trying to control my direction. Let-go blew through me like a welcome breeze.

It seems to me that let-go is not something we can *do*. It comes as a gift at a ripe moment. When we lose our grip and everything falls apart, we are stunned at what appears out of the wreckage. The very thing we were trying to bring to ourselves—in this case, an acceptance of myself and my life— was actually, through our efforts, being pushed away.

And a deeper let-go was yet to come.

At first, coming home from the emergency ward, there was pain. Then there was guilt (luckily the other people involved were not hurt); then there was tremendous self-doubt; then there was depression.

I wallowed around in a bog of self-recrimination for a few

painful days, until at last I was able to go out for a walk. It was a warm, drizzly day in May. I walked into town, alone.

There was the world in all its glory. Just as I had left it, but more intense, more vibrant, more real.

The body was shaky as "she" ambled through this brilliant rainy-day world. "She" knew something that the swirling mind did not: This had been a close call. The body had turned over her left shoulder and saw Death standing there. "She" now knew the fragility of the thread that connects her to life. And "she" was not afraid; "she" had embraced her vulnerability.

The mind, silenced by the shock of being in the world again, listened. And the body spoke: "We are still together, my dear, but this will not always be so. You will not always have the opportunity to see through these eyes, hear through these ears, feel through this heart.

"And see how the world goes on without you. Your efforts are not what keeps the universe afloat. Both your mistakes and your achievements are smaller than you think.

"The ego's tense, short-sighted evaluations of the moment have blinded you. You are here, now, alive. Don't miss it!"

And there is yet another layer. The accident has been like peeling an onion down to its empty center. After a few glorious days of lessons from the body, its wisdom began to fade behind the din of the mind revving up again. The mind's admonitions and calculations were harder to take seriously now, though; and I began to search for a way to make a permanent space for the body, its wisdom, and—most importantly—its death to live in me.

Wandering through a bookstore, a book called to me from the shelf. It was a recent compilation of J. Krishnamurti's talks, *On Living and Dying.* I opened to a question by a student at Rajghat, India, in 1954, "Why do we fear death?"

With deep thirst I drank his answer. It is actually a small, simple instruction for keeping death and its guidance alive in us. He said:

"... if we know how to die each day, then there is no fear. ..."

"We do not know how to die because we are always gathering, gathering, gathering. We always think in terms of tomorrow: 'I am this and I will be that.' We are never complete in a day; we do not live as though there is only one day to be lived. . . .

"If somebody told you that you were going to die at the end of the day, what would you do? Would you not live richly for that day? . . .

"If we live one day and finish with it and begin again another day as if it were something new, fresh, then there is no fear of death. To die each day to all the things that we have acquired, to all knowledge, to all memories, to all struggles, not to carry them over to the next day—in that there is beauty. . . ."

I turned back to the photo on the cover of the book. The weathered face (Krishnamurti was nearly ninety when it was taken) showed no effort to arrange itself for the camera. Inside his eyes was an easy, expansive emptiness; he had stopped his gathering, gathering, gathering long ago. Letting death take him daily, there was nothing left to fear. A hurricane wind could blow inside him, and it wouldn't stir a single leaf.

M: *Motherhood*

I used to believe you were
unknowing,
Unknowing of how it was for me,
As if you were never the blossom
trying to become the tree.

—Sumanas,
"*Mother's Day Poem,*" 1995

When I gave birth to Sumanas, I remember squeezing my eyes shut and focusing so intensely that I felt something of my deepest self being pushed down a long, dark tunnel. Every cell of me was given to the task; when, at last, excited voices began to reach me through the darkness. I opened my eyes to see where I had landed and found—lying in the large, gloved hands of a masked stranger—a tiny, wet, squalling human being.

In tremendous surprise I shouted, "Look! A baby!"

Everyone laughed, and so did I. But my surprise was authentic. Who would have believed? All this, and a baby, too. The sisterhood between mother and daughter is not contrived. They are born on the same day.

Mother. Say the word and listen. Slow it way down and feel the sound move around in your mouth: M-M-M-O-O-TH-TH-ERR. *It is a very sensual word, rich with vibrations in the lips, the hollow of the mouth, the teeth:* M-M-M-O-O-TH-TH-ERR.

The mmm *sound, with which we begin, is universal in its meaning. In documentaries we see tribesmen meeting anthropologists, and we hear a lot of "mmm"-ing, heads bobbing up and down:* mmm *means yes; very good; I understand; and, of course, delicious. I have heard that the names for mother in every language begin with this sound:* mmm.

So we begin our exploration into the mother with mmm—*saying yes; this is good; this is warm, soft . . . and delicious. The rest of the word also has a meaning on its own: "other." Adding the* mmm *indicates that this is not just any other, this is the first other, this is the* mmm *other; this one's delicious.*

"Other." Let's listen to it sound by sound. Uh *is the first.* Uh *rounds out and fills up the cave of the mouth. We are full with* uh.

Now th. *It is a strong sound, full of vibration. A thin jet stream of air is allowed to pass between the tongue and the teeth and sets the whole mouth rattling. As we all know, there is more to mother than that delicious fullness we get suckling at her breast. This is a powerful energy:* th! *And we know it when we see a mother letting loose in protection—or in discipline—of her child. Every mother has a tiger inside.*

Mother ends in er—*the sound of an engine, ready for takeoff.* Roaring, revved, *and* ready. *At her healthiest, a mother's essence contains the full spectrum from soft nurturance to fiery tigress. Again and again, she will need that fiery roar as she delivers her greatest gift—in regular increments, compassionate kicks beyond the nest. Her* roar *is our cue that we are* ready *for the next solo flight. It's time to* rev *our engines and start flapping those wings again. No time to wallow in self-doubt. Suddenly we are airborne, reveling in newfound freedom. Our chests expand; our hearts have more breathing room— someone is trusting us to fly on our own.*

In the early days of writing this book, I shared the idea with a few friends, who began to play the game themselves— choosing a topic for each letter of the alphabet and connecting it to a transformative life-story. My friend Abhi wrote a long playful letter of this genre, warning me emphatically: Do not use motherhood for the letter *M!* There were so many other great choices: moonlight, magic, miracle, meditation.

I understand Abhi's warning. The world of motherhood is wrought with pain and sorrow. The mother lives in the war-torn border town between her child's natural wildness and society's unrelenting demands. She often gets crushed from both directions. And, at the very least, she must witness, in absolute helplessness, the inevitable fall from innocence.

But from the very beginning, I knew I would have to go

into the whole sticky mess. What other situation has been so humbling, so surprising—so demanding of truth?

From the thousands of humorous, painful and touching incidents that life with children provides daily, I chose this story because it taught me about stepping back and trusting something larger to step in. It was one of the more powerful occasions of motherhood when yet another psychic umbilical cord is cut. The mother is urged to let the child wander a little farther into the world beyond her. Perhaps that world is not as hostile as she imagines. We haven't named our planet "Mother Earth" for nothing:

Appropriately, it was Mother's Day, 1988. Sumanas, age twelve, and DP, nine, met me in the afternoon at San Diego's Seaport Village, where I had worked in the morning. We were looking forward to celebrating the rest of the day together.

With nothing particular in mind, we meandered through the tourist shops, looking for fun. First we visited the hat shop, one of our all-time favorite places. We tried on almost every hat in the store, oohing, ahhing and laughing at one another. DP went for romance, always picking 1940 styles with rhinestones, bows and netting. I was drawn to the dramatic: large brims and feathers. Sumanas always had a taste for the absurd. She emerged from behind a post wearing a lobster-shaped piece of Day-Glo red foam, claws dangling before her eyes, laughing her famous rowdy laugh.

When we had exhausted all possibilities at the hat store, we went to a toy shop and bought a Frisbee, which we tossed around on a patch of grass outside the shop. None of us were very good at it, and even though the grass felt good on our bare feet, we tired quickly and soon agreed that it was time for refreshments. Since it was Mother's Day, I got to pick the place.

I chose a bookstore/cafe, and the girls enthusiastically agreed. The cafe was known for the most glamorous hot chocolate in Seaport Village, served in tall glass mugs with a mountain of whipped cream and chocolate shavings on top.

As we were looking for a place to sit and organize our plan of attack, one of the girls discovered tables upstairs on a balcony, which overlooked the bookshelves and coffee bar. We climbed the stairs and found a table away from it all, at the top of the world.

I was content to sit peacefully for a moment and take in the view of the buzzing crowd below, but Sumanas and DP were eager to taste the chocolate and whipped cream.

"We'll get it!" Sumanas suggested brightly. "It's Mother's Day. You sit here and we'll take care of everything."

DP was in passionate support of the plan. She helped me off with my jacket and took the wallet from my purse. "I'll do the paying," she offered. As self-appointed family treasurer, DP loved to count, arrange and spend the money in my wallet.

With that, they were off, leaving me happily "above it all."

When they appeared in line at the coffee bar, I looked down on them from an intriguing point of view. They had left me on another plane. I was out of sight, out of mind. I could watch them without the usual mother-prompted self-consciousness.

Even if you have not been a mother yourself, probably you have witnessed it. A mother watching her children at the swimming pool: "Watch *this*, Mommy!" "Look at *ME!*" "Mom, Mom! Watch me, Mom!"

But on this particular Mother's Day afternoon, I was graced with a welcome respite from that anxious place where no mother has enough eyes, or enough patience, to give everybody the attention they crave. Sighing, I settled into watching.

Seeing DP and Sumanas anew—not as *my* children but as children of the world—was quite touching. How bright and lively they looked in that line of "grown-ups." They danced around, pulling on one another, pointing at things, whispering in each other's ears and laughing. Their freshness to this planet was palpable.

Hundreds of animated gestures later, the girls arrived at the counter to place their order. I watched as coffee, cookies and cakes began to appear on the tray before them. At last, two mountainous glass mugs of hot chocolate—the Himalayas of the cafe—were placed on the tray. The girls looked at one another with large eyes and laughter as they proceeded to the cash register. As DP was counting out the money, Sumanas lifted the tray.

Suddenly the details of the scene below were played out in

slow motion. The tray was totally unbalanced by weight—all the liquid on one end. As Sumanas lifted the tray, her eyes wandered off in another direction—daydreaming or taking in some fascinating detail.

I saw the whole event before it actually happened, as mothers are genetically programmed to do. But now my position "above it all" seemed to be a horrible disadvantage. I could not jump in and take over as I had done instinctively countless times before.

I considered standing up and shouting over the balcony, but I could see that this would throw Sumanas's head in yet another direction, adding to the accidental components rather than subtracting from them. Helplessly I watched—my first training for the girls' adolescence that waited, invisible to all of us, around the next bend.

And the Himalayas came down. One of the mountainous hot drinks spilled all over Sumanas, who was, incidentally, wearing one of my favorite sweaters, the sleeves rolled three times to give access to her hands.

Chaos! Tremendous chaos! Everyone in the near vicinity awoke from his or her respective daydream and focused attention on the scene. A very tall man took the tray in his hands, one boy at the counter offered towels, a woman appeared to check for burns and minister to emotional wounds. Sumanas cried big, noisy tears.

It was all happening very quickly. I continued to watch.

Someone came with a mop. The counter was wiped clean. The cakes and cookies were salvaged, and the tray was exchanged for a new one. Upon it were placed a new cup of coffee and two new hot chocolates peaked with virgin snow. DP finished at the cash register, putting the change into the coin purse of the wallet. Sumanas gathered herself together and lifted the tray again, this time with laser focus.

I watched as she walked, as if on a tightrope through the crowd. Then she disappeared beneath me.

A few minutes later, DP and then Sumanas, whose face was dark with the heavy tale, arrived at our table. She gingerly set the tray down, not spilling a drop. She told of the misadventure in short breaths: "I spilled the hot chocolate. It got all over me. And all over your favorite sweater . . ." And falling into her chair, the dam broke again: tears and tears and more tears.

"I ruined your Mother's Day!" she sobbed.

I could only hold her and laugh. "You didn't ruin anything," I told her. "I'm having a wonderful time with you both today. I'm glad you weren't hurt. The sweater is only a piece of cloth."

I actually wanted to thank her, but how could I explain to a child the gift I had just received? Before this lesson would have meaning for Sumanas, she would have to be a mother herself. I had come to a point in my career as "parent" where I could see that there is another mother to whom we must, bit by bit, entrust our children.

In the pageant for which I was given a front-row balcony seat, an abundant supply of hands and hearts emerged from a roomful of "strangers." Although the impulse had passed through me to run downstairs after the disaster—make apologies for the children, carry the tray upstairs myself—a certain wisdom had overtaken my "motherly urges."

A new understanding was dawning in me that it was necessary and good for the mother to ultimately lift her protective wing, allowing her children to swim out into the world. This act brings an important message to the fledglings:

"This is *your* world. You are a part of it. You don't need a protector or a mediator. Life is a wonderful teacher and guide. . . . And, believe it or not, she is always on your side."

N: *Not-Knowing*

As for me, all I know is that I know nothing.

—Socrates

When Bodhidharma, the unpredictable Indian mystic and in the lineage of Mahakashapa (one of Buddha's close disciples), first arrived in China, the Chinese Emperor arranged a meeting. Emperor Wu presented himself to the eccentric monk, highlighting his contributions to the growth of Buddhism in China: "I have built many temples and helped to spread the Buddha's message throughout the land. . . . What will be my reward in Heaven?"

Bodhidharma looked at the monarch through his famous bulging eyes and roared: "Heaven? All these works were motivated by selfishness—to reserve yourself a special place in Paradise. Your reward is in Hell."

Shaken by this dismal summation of his lifework, Emperor Wu countered: "And who are *you* to make such sweeping judgments? Who are *you?*"

Bodhidharma laughed at the question and simply answered: "I don't know!"

Not-knowing. Through what uncharted sea does this sound take us?

Not. Let's listen to the sound of our first word. We begin with N. Making the sound of n closes the outer ear. No! eNough! We push back the outer world and enter ourselves with n.

Ot. Aht. Our next sound is ah, the sound of relaxed discovery:

Ah! Ears closed to the outer world, we relax and discover an innerworld. Now, bringing aliveness to our relaxed state, comes the tangy sound of t.

Alone, relaxed and alive in our inner world, we are ready to enter the land of knowing.

Our first sound is silent: k. *There is more to this word than meets the ear. This silence is the hidden secret of the word we are about to enter—the unspeakability of true knowing.*

Now, as we enter the audible part of the word, there is a surprising twist: in sound, the word is identical to "no-ing," "nay-saying."

When we "know" something, are we really negating it? Have you heard yourself saying in an argument, "I KNOW that!"? What are we really doing when we say we know someone or something? Are we not bringing a preconceived notion to the unique moment, therefore missing its freshness?

Not-knowing, then, is ending our habitual nay-saying to life's continual rebirth. It opens us, two negatives making a positive.

But let's continue on the sound voyage. With "not" we have come inside and are waiting with alertness. Noing—*With an ear-closing* n *we dive even deeper into ourselves, to the very center where we are round and whole and fresh:* o.

Now "ing," the suffix of action. From our cool, clear center, we rise to i, *a sound that vibrates between the eyes. According to the ancient Indian map of human energy, this spot between our eyes is called the "third eye," the seat of clear vision. We can see things from here that otherwise evade us. Having sunk so deeply into ourselves, perhaps we can see the world without prejudgment.*

*Ng. We travel down from the third eye past the ears (*n*) and end in the throat:* g. *In the Indian energy map, the throat is the center of truth. Perhaps only now, when we have ended our journey through "knowing" is it possible to speak truth: not-knowing—the deepest truth, the ultimate wisdom.*

A moment of not-knowing was my meditation master Osho's parting gift to me. It will be helpful for understanding this story if I explain my relationship to Osho, as best I can, in Western terms: He is the light of my life. I do not consider myself his follower, and I do not try to imitate him or his life. He has been for me a flesh-and-blood example of a complete human being, someone who has become whole.

Although I had very few face-to-face moments with Osho, my relationship to him was intimate—a word coming from the Latin word *intimus*, meaning innermost. Inexplicably, I felt loved in his presence, even though I was often in an auditorium with thousands of others. Love is never explainable, but the heart experience I had around Osho was most mysterious. Once I wrote a poem about it:

> My heart is filled with such love—
> Is it mine for you
> or yours for me?
> I cannot tell.

And thus, being with him took me back to an uncomplicated childhood feeling when I felt loved for no special reason. Back to when I had an imaginary playmate, who lived more inside me than out.

It was Poona, India. The date: January 1990. Osho had been sick for several years and the time he was able to spend with us had progressively decreased. At first, there were occasional days when he could not give his nightly discourse. He would joke about these absences, telling us that he had to "pretend" to be sick once in a while so we could learn to be on our own.

In late spring of 1989 the discourses stopped. Now Osho would come to the meditation hall very briefly in the evening, to greet us and to sit with us in silence. Sometimes too weak even for this visit, he would send a message that he was sitting with us in his room and that it was good for us to learn to be with him in this way.

As time went on, many of us began to notice that Osho made less and less personal eye-contact when he came upon the podium and greeted all of us in the auditorium. He seemed to look beyond us. He seemed to be indicating that our relationship to him was changing, that it was time to go deeper within ourselves, to find the source of love inside.

A few days before January 19, 1990, I was warming myself

in the morning sun on the back porch of Mirdad, the ashram building where I worked as staff writer for the newspaper. My friend Nartana stood on the steps, expressing her concern over Osho's failing health. I can still see her tears glistening in the bright Indian sun. "I'm afraid he's going to leave us," she whispered.

For the past ten years, this had been one of my own greatest fears. I did not find Osho at a very convenient time in my life. My children were very young when I first went traipsing off to India to meet him. Even my closest friends urged me to postpone the trip until the girls had grown up a bit. But experiencing the deaths of loved ones, I had seen that the window between two people closes very quickly, often without warning. I wanted to be sure to get to him before that window closed.

In planning each subsequent visit, I faced the same urgency again: that he would leave unexpectedly before I got to him. I always felt his dying before me was inevitable, so I carried a deep wish in my heart that whenever his time came, I would be blessed enough to be there.

I was surprised then, when I heard myself saying: "Oh, Nartana, he's going to outlive us all!" The statement reflected something that had happened without my noticing. The fear of losing the master had left; perhaps the master himself had stolen it! I remember those particular months at the ashram as a light inward time for me—writing, watching the birds, often choosing to be alone. And curiously, along with this relaxation, laughter was becoming my climate. In fact, on the evenings when Osho did arrive at the podium, his face beaming, all of us dancing with joy, I would often be caught in an unexpected, childlike spell of laughter.

On the night of January 18, Osho did not come to greet us. But in the videotaped discourse we watched, I heard him saying that there was never a need to make our journey a grim affair, that we always had the freedom to celebrate: paint, dance, sing and meditate; be joyous even in the darkest night.

The next day, I was once again standing on the Mirdad steps with Nartana, feeling inspired by the discourse. A layer of self-doubt had been washed away—perhaps it was okay to live and to create even though I wasn't a "finished product"!

A colleague overheard part of our conversation and asked me to clarify what I was saying. She was known for efficiency at the newspaper, while I was regarded as the artistic dreamer—and all the usual tensions that weave themselves between these two roles were woven between us.

When this friend heard my ecstatic reclaiming of artistic license, her lid blew off. "Prartho, that's your problem, not your insight!" she bellowed. "We all have to work hard to get out of our imaginations and back to the truth!"

She stormed off, and Nartana and I went our separate ways (I with a little less bounce). Once again I felt the rock of self-doubt weighing on my heart. Besides that, I was in a lot of physical pain with severe menstrual cramps. The urge to be alone got stronger. I went to the afternoon meditation, met my daughter for tea, and then decided to go home for the evening. Since Osho hadn't come the night before, he probably wouldn't be there tonight—a good night to be with myself. I packed up my things and walked out the gate.

I went on foot, taking the back way home. It was rare for me to be on the streets at this time of day; in my many years with Osho I had rarely missed an evening discourse. It felt as though I was entering another world, one that had gone on for centuries before I came. I watched as children were called to dinner, women swept their doorsteps, tea vendors and food merchants set up for the evening. The flowers sent out their fragrances on the dusk-breeze; dogs sighed and settled; people walked slower; the air grew gentle.

Home at my flat, I tiptoed past my apartment-mate, Niranjan, who was in the shower, knowing he would be leaving soon. I lay on my bed for a while, then went to sit on the tiny verandah off my room. I closed my eyes and joined the meditators in the ashram meditation hall a few blocks away.

Our nightly meditations opened with music and dancing, which started gently and built to a peak as Osho approached the auditorium. When he finally appeared on the marble podium, giggling with delight at our enthusiasm, we broke into several jubilant cries of "Osho!" We sang his name as a young lover might shout his beloved's name from the rooftops.

From my understanding of prayer (a concept I have considered much since it is what my name Prartho means), this light-hearted celebration was a prayer in the true sense of the word: In the dancing and shouting, we joyfully emptied ourselves, so when the silence of meditation came, there was room for it inside us.

Soon I heard the familiar shouting of "Osho!"—shouts so loud and clear as they came to me on the verandah that I felt as though I were in the hall.

Then came the silence. I listened. With the exception of a few screeching tropical birds, the earth was still. After sitting silently for some time, I was surprised by an urge to get up and play my guitar.

I played and sang every song I knew until I was empty. Then I crawled into bed with a book on Zen, read a short while and went to sleep.

I awoke with the sun, feeling refreshed. After a quick shower I went to leave, but found the door to our apartment padlocked from the outside—the most common security system in India. Niranjan hadn't known I was inside when he left the night before, and he had not come home, probably spending the night at his girlfriend's flat.

Oh well, I thought, someone will show up eventually. I put on some music and danced for my morning meditation (dance, a form of meditation in many traditions from Hindu to Sufi, has always been my favorite). Then I sat on the verandah with a cup of coffee. While I was sitting there, a woman came to hang laundry in the courtyard below my window. I threw down my keys and she let me out.

It was about nine o'clock in the morning. The sun was already above us, but the street was surprisingly quiet. I stopped for a quick breakfast pastry at the German Bakery, an Indian establishment designed for the Western palate. A newspaper was spread out in front of the man at the checkout counter. I glanced down to read the headline: "RAJNEESH IS DEAD," it pronounced.

For much of his life, Osho was known as Rajneesh, but

signifying that his work was entering a new phase, he had dropped that name more than a year before. He had gone nameless for several weeks, until his disciples chose to call him Osho. So this headline seemed to be old news. Of course Rajneesh is dead. He's been dead for a long time now, I thought.

But something didn't quite fit. The press never took interest in what Osho was actually saying; when he dropped his name and declared a new phase of his work, they had taken little note. "Rajneesh is dead? What's that supposed to mean?" I heard myself asking the man at the counter.

"You mean you don't know?!" The man looked at me incredulously.

No, I didn't know. I stood there, stripped naked by his question.

"We burned him last night," the man told me, his eyes still wide with disbelief at my ignorance.

I said a stupid thing then, in perfect tune with that ignorance. "You're kidding," I said—the American expression I used so much in growing up. "I don't want to believe you. This can't be real." And I ran off in tears.

I wrestled with questions about denial for a long, long time. Maybe I *did* know. Several friends challenged me, reminding me of my reputation for being sensitive and intuitive, even psychic. Surely I knew something. In a great act of avoidance, had I managed to hide away in my room in order not to face the master's death?

The part of me that likes to think I "know things" lived with the guilt of this notion for many years after Osho left. I had "known" and I had escaped and missed my chance to be with him at his moment of departure, to dance at his funeral pyre.

But the truth is that all I heard inside myself that night was a strong call to be alone. I had been sitting on the verandah while my apartment door was locked. Friends who came to find me saw the padlock outside and assumed I wasn't there. My flatmate never came back. I was left alone.

I did not know.

It is a relief to admit this, to doff the mask of knowing.

"You mean you don't know?"

Yes, that's right, I don't know. Most of the time I don't know anything.

But once in the Indian morning sunlight with my friend Nartana, I *did* know something. I knew then, and I still know now, that he—his essence—will outlive us all.

O: *Osho*

*Unless you are ready to encounter yourself
you cannot become a disciple, because a Master
... can only help you to face yourself.*

—Osho, *The Mustard Seed*

Osho. You will hear this name slipping into and out of many of my stories. Osho's presence in my life has been the most mysterious miracle I have lived. He often told us that he was not really here, that he had left long ago, that what we saw in him was a reflection of ourselves.

As a child I had imaginary playmates. There was a boy and a girl, blond and athletic, who were twins. Their names were Jimmy and Judy, and they played normal children's run-around-the-yard games, which I often enjoyed but sometimes tired of. When boredom overtook me, I would find Churchy, a neutral-sexed elder—both male and female, or possibly neither. He (I used the male pronoun in its neutral sense) had a bald pate with long, curly hair. His main activity was watching. Sometimes we would talk about Jimmy and Judy. He was open to talking about anything. He was my best friend.

In the early days of finding Osho, I looked at his photo— long, curly hair; bald on top; intense, loving eyes—and gasped, "Churchy, is that you?" My best friend was back—the watcher, the one with whom I could talk over anything.

Osho, I am told, is a common name in Japan, almost equivalent to "Spiritual Grandfather." It is often found in children's books. The literal meaning I was given once—"The Blessed One, on Whom the Sky Showers Flowers"—seems like a mouthful for this dainty little word. Osho himself said that the name meant "the one who experiences the oceanic." It seems he was listening to the lesson of its sound. Let's dive in:

Osho. The first secret in this sound is that it both begins and ends with O, the letter and sound of whOleness.

O. The sound of zerO, of emptiness with its infinite possibilities. "O!" The exclamation of fullness. The sound of jOy. No wonder we call the Ocean, "Ocean."

In both Ocean and Osho the O's are followed by shhh. What an exquisite combination of sounds: o . . . shhh. With O we enter wholeness and wonder; with shhh we fall silent. We listen to the ocean's roar, to the cosmic song. "Shhh," listen. It works on the smallest of babies: shhh.

And if we listen deeply enough, we lose ourselves in the ocean; we become it. We disappear and only the o remains: o . . . shhh . . . o. Osho.

It is said that when the disciple is ready, the master appears. Life waits for the heat of our search to reach the boiling point so the clouds in our eyes can evaporate. Only then does Life arrange our meeting with a master. Before this, we would never recognize him. A certain earnest impatience, a *divine discontent,* is necessary for us to find the eyes that can see.

This is the story of one summer when the heat of my quest brought me to the boiling point . . . and eventually to Osho. These are the events that led to the master finding me:

For the first two summers after my mother died, I went to a yoga ashram in the mountains of Pennsylvania for teacher training. It was as much a retreat for sorting out the contents of my heart as it was an education.

During the first summer, I had gotten into a small battle with the head yogi over sex. He preached celibacy and even separated us by gender in the lecture hall. One day he was explaining his reasons for advocating the renunciation of sex: "Sex is just the release of tension," he said. "Really it's just a sneeze!"

"Sometimes sex is more than that!" I blurted out from my cushion on the floor in front of him. "Sometimes you go beyond yourself in sex. Your selfishness and ego disappear. I think sometimes you get very close to God in sex."

"It is true," he conceded and went on to explain, "for that very reason you must renounce it! This is God's challenge to you."

"But why would God do it that way?" I asked. I did not really believe there was a person on a cloud making rules, but my question about the spiritual life was intensely sincere. "Why would God give you a taste of Him and then say, 'Okay, now no more'?"

"That's just how He works. We become easily attached to things and we must give up all our attachments," was his reply.

I took his answer and mulled it over for quite a while, but I could not find a place inside where it resonated. I had heard similar advice about "giving up attachments" before, but the idea of this universe of tremendous possibility being created— only for us to give it up—seemed ridiculous. Surely we have come to this ocean to taste the salt, smell the air and tumble in the waves.

By the second summer my questions had gathered such force that I could barely contain them. I had been wondering since childhood at the strange, emotionally intricate, creative species of which I was a member. It had always disturbed me that the vast majority of people seemed to grow pale and dead with the years—as if the juice of life had leaked out of them. From the beginning I was convinced that we did not come here just to endure the trials of life. We were made for something wonderful, and I was going to find it.

For many years of my young adult life, I had used Western psychology as my light on the path. I was trained and worked as a Gestalt therapist, and I participated in almost every thera-peutic process available: from Bioenergetics to Rolfing, dreamwork to encounter groups. I became skilled in the arts of self-disclosure, catharsis and insight, but was only made more aware of another universe inside, which remained untouched by any of these methods.

At a certain point in the road, psychology's light, whose beam could only reach the veneer of my personality, became too dim. I had walked with death for a year and a half. I had seen my own end reflected in the eyes of my dying parents. I had given birth and saw how little was actually in my hands. I needed to know: Was there anyone who had gone beyond this brambled point on the path? Were there sighted ones among us in the land of the blind? I felt I needed only one example to stand as proof that something more was possible.

By the second summer, the fire in my belly was hot. Living in a tent at the edge of the property, I spent a lot of time alone with my questions, writing long, passionate journal entries. Every morning I awoke with fragments of intense dreams that pursued me in my sleep. Eventually there were nightmares about my life in the ashram—particularly about my relationship to the spiritual leader.

The leader was referred to as a "guru," which we were told was a Sanskrit word made up of *gu:* darkness and *ru:* light. Thus the guru brought light to darkness. The possibility stirred hope in me, but sometimes this man seemed to cast shadow, not light. In his presence I often sensed an undercurrent of deception.

So I lived in a kind of split-brain turmoil for the first month, halfheartedly taking part in the devotional rituals focused on the guru and, in my time alone, struggling with my distrust of him. Working and studying among devotees, I lived in the fear of being found out. When the nightmares surfaced, I knew I could no longer avoid my fears; I would have to confront them—and the guru—soon.

The ashram had grown so since the first summer, that now one had to stand in a long line before asking the guru a question through a microphone. Reminding myself of when I was nine years old trying to jump off the high dive at the Y, I walked up to, and back from, the line at the microphone for several days before I found the courage to get in line early enough and stay there until it was my turn. I stood in line for over an hour and—for better or worse—jumped.

I remember looking over the heads of several hundred people to the robed man on stage. My heart pounded so loudly that I could barely hear myself as, microphone in shaking hand, I began, "I'm not sure this will make any sense . . . but I'm having a lot of trouble with what goes on here. A lot of the time I don't feel I should be here at all. . . ." Then I broke into tears, feeling my tangle of hopes and fears coming out of hiding to parade themselves nakedly before the world.

After a few long moments of uncontrolled sobs, I loosely gathered myself and continued, "I especially have trouble with the feeling that you put yourself higher than everybody. I have nightmares about everyone bowing to you."

"I am not higher than you, but I am clearer than you. I am just a pipe—clear enough that the higher can come to you through me," I heard the man on stage saying through his own microphone. "I represent your own growth, that's why you are afraid of me. Someday this will make sense to you."

Although these words sounded like something a wiseman might say, the bell of truth did not sound. I thanked him, passed the microphone on, and returned to my seat, my questions drawing themselves back up inside me. Although the session continued, the voices got farther and farther away, and I went flying out the window into the summer-afternoon clouds.

At dinner I didn't sit in the dining area with the others, but took my tray to a solitary corner of the garden. I set my food down on the grass, and the tears came again.

I was so disappointed that nothing was resolved in exposing my doubts and fears, that I had not been delivered to a moment of truth. The fog seemed only more dense, and my hope that we humans were capable of living in the light was shrinking.

Lost and alone, I cried over my dinner until the tears finally subsided. I took a deep breath and looked out beyond the lake, beyond the trees, beyond the sky. A friend from teacher's training came and stood next to me then, joining me in my silence.

"I want to tell you something," she said, squatting next to me and balancing her tray in one hand. "The whole time you were talking at the microphone this afternoon, I kept thinking of this book *The Mustard Seed.* I kept thinking, 'She needs to read *The Mustard Seed.*' So I decided to tell you. It's a very strong book and I think it would help you with your questions."

When disappointment empties us, it seems we are more capable of hearing. I knew that I would find that book one day and read it.

Nothing more was said. We carried our trays back to the kitchen, where we said good night and went our separate ways.

Several months later, back home in Portland, Maine, I was browsing through the stacks of my favorite bookstore, when a title leapt off the shelf: *The Mustard Seed,* in bold yellow letters on a black spine.

My heart beat faster when I saw it. It was as though my destiny were standing there on the shelf. I took the book in my hand and turned it over to find a black-and-white portrait of its author on the cover. A confusion of fear and excitement arose in me as I heard myself saying, "Oh my God, it's him!" I wasn't sure what I meant by this at the time, but he looked eerily familiar.

I bought the book and brought it home. In my bedroom that night, I began to read. By the second page, tears were flowing. I ran for a pen and began to underline, circle, make stars in the margin: "I must remember these things!"

Even as I was urging my memory to take note, I felt the author was saying things I knew once but had somehow forgotten; it was as though he was giving voice to my most secret feelings.

The author, of course, was Osho—the one who would eventually be my impassioned guide in meditation, offering encouragement and methods for exploring the uncharted terrain of my heart and soul. It remains a mystery to me why my friend suggested this book. She herself never came to Osho, while for me the book opened a door into a world beyond my imaginings. And the yogi's role in my search is an even deeper mystery, for it was his apparent inability to provide me with guidance that led me directly to that which I had so long been seeking: a master of life.

"At the boundary of sight is the mustard seed, the smallest thing in the world of the visible . . . ," Osho tells us, reminding us that inside this tiniest of spheres is hidden the greatest of trees.

And so it was. The sincerity and persistence of my searching had broken open a tiny seed of possibility, and something new began to sprout. As a seedling is pushed by some invisible force through the earth, I felt myself being pushed to stand naked before several hundred people and ask for the truth.

Perhaps even when a seedling breaks through into her new world, she wonders if all her struggle was really worth it. The light is harsh; there is no soft, comforting earth around her. But soon the gardener arrives, giving water and encouragement. And, grateful for being found and nourished, the sprout begins to remember what she came for. She reaches for the stars.

P: *Poor*

꩜

It is not the man who has too little, but the man who craves more that is poor.

—Seneca, *Episulae ad Lucilium*

I am not a fan of poverty. Any romanticism about the "blessed poor" that I might have kept up my sleeve fell out upon first stepping off the plane in India and confronting a sea of emaciated people, clawing at the dirty window from outside the terminal. Living in India for many years, I have seen that poverty is perhaps the most ugly expression of human life on the planet.

There is nothing blessed about squalor, starvation, or the diseases they engender. Yet I am choosing the poor for my topic, because I find that it is not always clear who is who in the land of poverty and wealth. On the scale from rags to riches, there seems to be a paradoxical point where some who are apparently wealthy turn out to be immensely poor, and a few who seemingly have nothing shine forth as emperors. Perhaps you have seen it: paupers living inside the eyes of "rich men" and, once in a while, someone "poor" exuding immeasurable wealth.

Poor. What can be heard in this small, undemanding sound?
Poor: *It is a simple sound. Soft and round. Made of two basic sounds that easily slide together: P and oor.*
What great irony: oor is a golden nugget, the sound of wealth. The sound oo, what we make when we "Ooh and Ahh" over something valuable beyond words, is followed by R as in rich and rupee. In the world of sound, oor is pure gold, and here it is ushered in by P—a

delicate puff *of a sound:* pure, pretty, perhaps *even* prayerful. *The word "poor" comes in stocking feet, quietly leaving us with a treasure.*

What does this mean? Could it be that when we were first making words, there was something truly blessed about possessing little? When there were not so many of us, and the world was rich with fruits, game and space; when greed and fear had not yet carved the Great Divide between the Haves and the Have-Nots, perhaps to live simply, without the weight of possessions, was seen as the "quiet wealth." Perhaps this is what Jesus meant when he said the poor are blessed.

I don't know for sure. But this is what I hear in its sound.

One day I watched a very small boy lug a bucketful of very big rocks down the beach. Staggering beneath the weight of his treasure, he had a hard time keeping up with his family. The others, two grown-ups and a sister almost twice his size, swung their arms leisurely and chatted above his head.

Sometimes he would lag far enough behind that his presence would be missed, and someone would turn and nag him to come along. Once he became so engrossed in a seagull that he lost track of the bucket and spilled the biggest rock. He could not get a proper grip on the large round stone. Grunting and groaning, he attacked it from all directions with his little hands. No success.

At last his sister noticed that he was fighting a losing battle. She managed to pick up the stray and balance the bucket, which he continued to hold very tightly, while she plopped the rock back in. He smiled at her briefly, but, learning from his mistake, quickly brought his attention back to the bucket and resumed a zigzag path down the beach.

The boy got his fortune as far as the family umbrella. I don't know what became of it after that. But I remembered that boy as I was thinking over poverty and wealth. For a while at least, as those great, round, glistening rocks were being gathered, the boy was rich! By outrageous luck, the dragon was fast asleep when he came upon those immense jewels. He had found endless, unguarded treasure and carted away as much as his little body could hold.

But the moment comes . . . it may have come even before he

left the beach. If not then, in the months or years ahead. Someday, perhaps when he is packing up to move on, there will be a moment when our young Sisyphus will feel the weight of his wealth pushing him back down the hill into the valley of poverty. One day he will be fed up with hauling around the universe and long for the wealth of living lightly.

The moment will come. It has come for all of us—many times. Remember the migrant worker in the movie, *Tortilla Flat* who inherited a gold pocket watch? His friend looks at the inheritance and shakes his head.

That watch is the beginning of the end, his friend warns him. Now you're going to have something to worry about. You'll always be anxiously checking your pocket to see if it's fallen through a hole. You'll have to be on guard in a crowd and make sure that nobody steals it. One day it's going to break and you'll have to find the money to fix it. There's a whole bunch of misery in that little watch.

Next scene finds the two friends enjoying an expensive bottle of wine under a tree; the watch has been traded for the ephemeral: a summer afternoon rich in friendship.

Now I must confess as I write this: Today I am surrounded by my own collection of ocean-tumbled rocks that I gathered yesterday. After enough time of arm-swinging freedom, one longs for a few rocks in the pockets again. Perhaps the key to true wealth lies in a natural rhythm of gathering and letting go. Perhaps contentment lies in the freedom to wander on both sides of the moon—sometimes enjoying the cool, empty shade; sometimes the warm full sun.

My favorite moment with a rich, perhaps even blessed, "poor man" happened in India. I would like you to meet a fruit seller who knows something about living with gusto on the dark side of the moon:

The stretch of road outside the ashram is lined with Indian entrepreneurs selling carved Buddhas, Tibetan bowls, crystal jewelry, and brightly colored clothing. There are meditation cushions, grass floor mats, handmade drums, and bamboo bookshelves. Some vendors sell the less tangible: snake charming, magic shows, neck rubs, palm readings, songs. Quite a few sell fruit.

The fruit sellers hang together. Especially after the evening meditation, when folks are apt to be hungry for a little something sweet, the fruit sellers call out. They form a chorus, each with his or her own peculiar rhyme and rhythm. There are two women who have sat on this street, almost every night, for some fifteen years. One sings out a greeting before listing her wares—"Hello, Ma!"—her bangled arm raised high. "Orange? Grapefruit? Lee-mon today?"

The other is famous among ashramites for her droning song: "Papaya, papaya, papaya ... banana, banana ... orange, orange, papaya." Even when her inventory is small, the variations of her song are endless: "Banana, banana ... papaya ... banana, papaya ..."

Our story is about the third "regular" of Fruit Sellers' Row, a man of slight build who dresses entirely in white: white buttoned shirt, white *lunghi* wrapped around his thin brown legs, white Gandhi cap on his head. He does not sit on a blanket like the ladies. He has a bicycle with a large round basket, and he stands beside it. He is proud of his business, particularly the bicycle. Overall, one gets the feeling that he is happy to be here. When anyone passes, he beams. He is generous with his smile.

One balmy evening as I was strolling down the ashram road, I was especially enjoying the fruit sellers' chorus. I had grown quite fond of these three faces, and although I rarely bought fruit on the street, they greeted me as an old friend.

On this particular night, our man with the Gandhi cap and bicycle was singing like an opera star. He was at the far end of the row, but I could hear him above all the others, calling out a seemingly endless offering of fruits: "Pineapple, papaya, chicoo, or-r-range, mango, watermel*looon* ... !"

When at last I reached him, I found him smiling brighter than ever. Responding with my own biggest grin, I peered into his basket. I couldn't believe my eyes: empty but for two small lemons.

I looked up at him. Though he was still smiling, his body curled shyly.

"But you don't have any of that fruit!" I said, stating what was now obvious to both of us.

He broke into a great, mischievous laugh. And, of course, I joined him. He had caught me. Not in the way that we all usually fish, to see what we might get from the world of passersby. He had caught me in the net of his delight, in a joke on his own predicament. He had thrown that glittering lure to get me close enough to share a bit of his ridiculous wonder.

I felt rich; what to say about him? I have never known a wealthier man.

Q: *Questions*

I have answered three questions and that is enough.

—Lewis Carroll, *You Are, Old Father William*

Questions are the arrows our mind sends out on its quest to penetrate the unknown. But for every answer an arrow brings down, a dozen more question marks fall from the sky.

Anyone traveling with a small child can witness the mind as tireless archer:

"Why isn't the train moving?"

"We are waiting."

"Why are we waiting?"

"Other people have to get on."

"Where are the other people? Where do the other people come from? Where are all the other people going?"

And if you succeed in answering those, it goes on: "What is that light for? How come there are so many tracks? Why is that bell ringing?"

But once I met a child who had traded all her arrows for one golden spear. In fact, it was only yesterday.

Yesterday I put a silver star on my forehead and set up shop as a "psychic reader" at a local festival. I was giving sample readings. Readee's choice: palm (a look into one's karmic life-predicament), stones (perspectives on the present-life passage), or cards (questions answered).

Since the readings were free samples, a waiting pool soon formed; its most eager constituent was a young girl about eight years old with rosy cheeks and yellow hair. She stood there for almost an hour, her eyes glowing with intensity.

After every reading I would nod for her to come, but three times in a row an adult would appear from behind me and give testimony to being next: "I have been here longer than she has. I saw when she arrived."

Usually I doubted the adult and argued on behalf of the rosy-cheeked girl, but each time she bowed back with a shy smile, none of the eagerness in her eyes diminished.

At last it was her turn. When I presented the choices—palm, stones or cards—she said with great certainty, "I want the cards ... there is just one thing I want to know."

So that was what held her so patiently in line. She was carrying a question. An urgent question. And I was to be the Oracle. I took a deep breath and brought myself as totally into the moment as I could. "Okay," I began as I pulled a deck of cards from my bag, "what is your question?"

"I want to know ..." She leaned forward and, looking me straight in the eye, almost whispered, "How can I find out who I am?"

The arrow of her question pierced my heart. Such wide-eyed innocence addressing the question that most of us run from all the way to our graves.

As I looked out at her through the tears that had just sprung into my eyes, she explained further, "This question is there all the time. I can't find an answer to it. Sometimes I think of something I might be, but then again, I don't think so."

I had her cut the cards and then fanned them out on the table. But before I told her to choose any, I leaned forward until we were almost nose to nose. "This is a wonderful question, maybe the most important question anyone can ask. The fact that this is your question shows how very intelligent you are," I said. I had fallen in love. If I had been in India, I would have touched her feet.

She chose five cards, as I instructed, and I began to explain their placement in the spread. "This card will tell us what the 'issue' is," I said.

She put her hand to the side of her mouth and told me a

secret, "I am not from America; I do not understand the word 'issue. . . .' "

Strange, I had not noticed a foreign accent, but now she explained to me that she was from Holland. And so, slowly, in the most elementary language, we went through the "answer" to her question.

The issue was "past lives." She shook her head no: This word was not in her vocabulary.

"Reincarnation?"

"No."

So I explained the theory of transmigration of the soul, and lights flashed in her eyes.

"I have not heard of that, but I have felt it in myself," she told me. "You see, this is the thing: If I think who I am is a young, blonde girl from Holland, I think, well, maybe I also was an old man with dark hair the time before, and maybe later I'll be different again."

We continued with the reading, but halfway through she urgently pulled on the sleeve of my kimono and confessed, "Sometimes it is terrible, this question. Sometimes I can't even sleep at night. And then I just pray that the question will go away, but it doesn't."

Now I felt the agony of this child with the big question, and I searched for some way to reduce the weight of it. I took out another deck, the one I use for my own questions—each card depicting a spiritual story—and asked her to choose one. The card that she drew told the story of a samurai approaching a Zen master with his own burning question, "Tell me, Master, what is Heaven and what is Hell? Show me: Where are the gates?"

The master cleverly provokes the samurai to pull his sword and then explains, "In this moment you are standing at the gates of Hell." Seeing the point, the samurai returns his sword to its sheath and the master sighs, "Ah, the gates of Heaven."

When I finished telling the story we both fell silent. Finally the message I was to give came to me. "I think this card is telling you to stop fighting your question. It is a good question and because it is a good question, it will probably take a long, long time to find the answer. It might even take your whole life! But it will be a good life with this question. Just let it be there. Let it be your friend. . . ." I looked at her hopefully. "Does that make any sense?"

"Very much!" she exclaimed. "Thank you!" She slid from the seat and ran off, her question bobbing behind her like a yellow balloon.

Question. Into what regions do we fly on its sound?
Que. Kwe—*as the dictionary writes the sound.* Kw—*feel the mouth as it stretches the crisp* k *sound from deep in its hollows out through the pushed-forward lips: the* QU*iver is set in place.* E—*now the lips stretch back: the bow is pulled taut.*
Stion. S-s-s, *the sound of graceful movement, of* snaking, sliding, skating: *the arrow is* S*ent flying. Until it reaches* T, *a* terse, *defini*T*e sound: the arrow hits its mark.*
Ion. Ion *is a turning back to* n—*a sound that vibrates out into the ears, leaving us in the privacy of our own interiority.*
All questions lead to home. To that calm pool inside where no question arises, and neither is there a ripple of an answer.

Gertrude Stein, the philosopher/poet, was known for her ability to generate questions that no one else had ever thought to ask. Questions begetting questions, until on her deathbed she squeezed the hand of her friend, Alice B. Toklas, and, with typical fierceness, asked, "What is the answer?"

Nothing but silence filled the room. No answer coming, Gertrude is said to have laughed and uttered her last words: "In that case, what is the question?"

An important personal message about life's questions and answers came to me in a dream: Years of wandering through the mazes of higher education left me with a recurring anxiety dream about examinations. In these dreams I have totally forgotten about a course when I hear about the final exam. Sometimes I am actually taking the test when it occurs to me that I have read or heard nothing of the material. A dream I had the week after a trip to Jamaica, is one of those.

We are sitting at tables under a tent. Patches of sky, sea and garden are visible through large openings at either end. I have become lost in the breezes blowing outside those openings when I hear the voice of a tall, black, Jamaican man in the corner, telling us how much time is left for us to answer the questions.

I anxiously look down at the paper in front of me and find two essay questions with large spaces for writing beneath them. The first question asks about the history of the Jamaican railroad. I know nothing about the Jamaican railroad. In fact, I didn't even know that there was one, but as the test monitor announces time running out, I force my hand to the paper and begin to write.

I find it very difficult to formulate any thoughts. I fall into what is easiest for me: storytelling. Soon I realize I am deeply involved in a story about a small girl who lives by the sea . . . and not a single train has chugged by! The Jamaican calls time once more, and I know if I am to get to question number two, I'll have to leave this strange response as it is.

I move on to the second question, but no sooner have I read a few words than I have lost them. I can't focus or make sense of the question. My impulse is to fake it: Write *something*. Write *any*thing! But the pen does not go to the paper, and eventually the Jamaican calls "Stop!"

The test is over. Bent beneath my sense of failure, I bring my test paper to the corner where the Jamaican is sitting, his chair tilted back, his hands laced together as a headrest, white straw hat tilted down toward his nose. He is the picture of Jamaican "soon-come" relaxation.

Frustration pouring out from every cell, I toss the paper on his desk. He laughs.

"Don't be in such a hurry to judge yourself on this test," he tells me, lifting his hat to reveal the mischief in his eyes, and flashing a smile that shows almost every one of his white teeth. "There are many right answers on this test."

I am not consoled. Maybe in some remote universe there is a connection between a small girl at the seashore and the history of the Jamaican railroad, but that gaping hole beneath the second question . . . "For the second question I didn't put *any*thing," I tell him, my face scrunching into a prune.

He laughs again as he rocks back on his chair and happily informs me, "That's one of the right answers!"

R: Remembering

I wasn't conscious
day or night.
I thought I knew who I was,
but I was you.

—Rumi, *Open Secret*

At the heart of the human predicament is forgetfulness. A forgetfulness so deep that we can not even remember what it is we have forgotten. Did we leave something behind—like an umbrella or a pair of glasses? Is it some maxim—like the law of life—that has escaped us? Or have we forgotten some very essential thing—like who we are?

We don't know. We can only feel the itch of it and a vague sense that if we could just remember, everything would fall into place.

Forgetfulness is an important part of the Indian version of the human story. A story that begins with a universe of creative, compassionate light. For the sheer fun of it, this loving intelligence sends millions of sparks of itself into form. And a great drama ensues. In Sanskrit the drama is called *Lila*—"the play."

Passion for experience moves the spark through form: from stone to moss to fern to tree to eagle to mosquito to elephant to man. Because of the light's love of freedom, each spark's progression is unique. It moves in its own way and its own time, playing all its roles with such conviction that the drama is fit for a king.

At some point, however, the spark realizes it has lost its way. It cannot remember where it came from or how to get back. Having reached as far into the darkness as it can bear, it suffers the incomparable pain of separation.

It is here that the spark has entered human form. We humans are as far away from the source as sparks get. We have forgotten totally who we are.

Now motivated by a new desire, longing for the light, we take on a series of human incarnations. Slowly our desires evolve from the avoidance of pain and experience of pleasure to dissolving into compassion, until at last we awaken from the dream. We remember who we are.

Remember. Can its sound, perhaps, shed light on the path that leads home?

Remember. This is one of those full-circle words whose beginning and end meet in the same letter, giving the sound a roundness. *We begin and end in the* richness *of an* R, *while the middle of the word mumbles with* M's *and a* B. *Let's take the sound journey along this circular path:*

R *rolls in like thunde*R. *We are alive and g*Rowling *when the pure energ*EE *of a long* E *zooms in, and we're off!*

This electric start delivers us into a rolling landscape of M's: mem. *Now the world around us hu*MM*s; perhaps we are even lulled to sleep, forgetting the raw storm of energy out of which we were born.*

But all dreams come to an end, and as this one does, we are met by B, *our most nonserious letter—leading a parade of words like* baby, babble, *and* bingo. B *bounces in and we playfully ride it back to* R.

In this—as in all circles—where we are going, where we came from, and where we are, is all the same place. Really, it is impossible to get lost. Remembering this, the whole thing comes round.

This is the story of one of the most delicate moments of my life. It came and went like a breeze, but I have not been the same since:

By the time I was in graduate school, I had learned the ways of doubt and applied them to everything. Instead of hearsay, I put my trust in experience and, as a result, my experience of life grew rich. Working as an intern at the University Counseling Center, I participated in as many growth groups and body-oriented therapies as my days could hold. I was living a philosophy once maximized by a colorful American Sufi teacher, Sufi Sam: "Thinking is stinking, but the feel is real."

Exploring the foothills of body and soul, many things opened. I felt alive again! All of Life's doors and windows were ajar.

It was in this climate that I began to wonder about the Mystics. I had no knowledge about the mystical traditions of the world, only a vague sense that some people spoke of a larger experience. Now I began to consider that this might be possible. And in the unlikely temple of a VW van, the light switch was accidentally touched, giving me the briefest glimpse of the inner room.

I had recently befriended a brilliant woman studying criminal law who called herself a Christian Mystic. Julia was wild, unconventional and funny. I loved her. She surprised me at every turn.

One night we planned to have dinner at a restaurant, which was an hour's drive away. My husband was already there when I arrived at Julia and David's from an all-day body/mind workshop. I had entered some profound states that day, and by now I was flying.

Julia and I climbed into the back of the VW van, where we were immediately consumed by the intense dialogue that spontaneously ignited whenever we met. This time I was questioning her about mysticism, still careful not to commit myself in any direction. She spoke eloquently, drawing from both East and West, telling stories in which Jesus seemed so human, I felt as though we could have had a beer with him.

Deep into our conversation Julia exposed the heaviness of her heart to me: "It worries me so, the direction this world is taking. . . ."

"Oh, Julia," I replied, "everything is moving along as it should; it's all going to be okay."

The sadness dropped from my friend's face as she looked at me with new eyes. "Why Gwen (which was the name I used then)," she exclaimed, beaming, "you have the faith!"

I do? I had never counted myself as one of The Faithful. Yet

I had just discovered a feeling inside that everything was going exactly as it should.

"Well, maybe I do have the faith. . . ." I conceded, but that was not enough. "What I really want is a mystical experience!"

I had recently come across Abraham Maslow's idea of the "mystical experience." Maslow found that some individuals (fewer than one percent of the population by his estimation) were self-actualizing—not only had they left neurosis behind, but they were capable of celebrating life in all its changes. Among the defining traits of these self-actualizers were frequent expeditions into the oceanic or mystical experience.

Hmmm. *An experience.* This was my language. But when the oceanic experience was explained as losing boundaries and melting into the universe, I found nothing in my own life to relate to. I felt poor.

Back in the backseat of the VW van, Julia looked at me and considered my request. Then she looked out the window and said, "Well, Gwen, one can seek the 'mystical experience' and still be agnostic, but once you have one, things are gonna change."

For some reason beyond me, this statement bypassed my mind and went directly into my belly. As I heard it, two eternally warring worlds slid together: one side filled with hope, goodness and angelic choirs; the other with darkness, despair, poverty and war. With their sliding together, a great sigh came out of me and a chill went up my spine. A tidal wave of a chill. A chill I could ride like a surfer.

As the wave gently settled in my skull, a light dawned. Not a bright blinding light, but a soft one—ultimately kind. Silently, without words, the light conveyed that all was well. No need for fear here; no need to strive, struggle or search. I was home.

On the shore of this experience, all was still but for one element of surprise: The place was *familiar*. Profoundly familiar. And although for some timeless time the mind had no thoughts, when finally it could speak again, its first words were, "This?! . . . This?! . ."

How did I ever forget this, I thought. Is this what they mean when people talk about God? This is the basic thing, the only thing, really. In fact, compared to this, everything else in life is a little weird.

As the light slowly retreated and I returned to the darkness of the van, I wondered how long I had been gone. But no one seemed to notice that I had left. The conversation continued as if nothing had happened at all. And although the compassionate light disappeared as unexpectedly as it had come, my landing was gradual and gentle. I found my social self mysteriously capable of conversing, while my being sat on a silent peak deep in my own interior.

It was some weeks before I told anyone what had happened. How to say it? "The war ended in my belly, a chill went up my spine, and I remembered something that I can't believe I could have forgotten (though, for the most part, I already have)?"

Eventually, I told the story here and there to intimates, mainly to remind myself of where I came from and where this strange journey just might be taking me. What awes me to this day is the simultaneous smallness and immensity of that moment—a moment that fit into the space between breaths, but, as Julia predicted, changed me forever. You see, no matter how entangled I become in the overgrown jungles of doubt, I continue to be haunted by the familiarity of that empty, loving light.

Even when everything else can be doubted, I cannot seem to doubt that I will come upon this light again, and when I do, I will laugh as I hear myself saying, "This?! . . . This?! . . . How did I ever forget this?"

S: *Sanity*

*With your white hairs
blowing all around,
how can I stay sane?*

—Swami Mouni,
Spontaneous Song to the Master

I recently got a letter from my little sister. We have just begun to correspond again after nearly a decade of silence. The two-page, handwritten letter was a distillation of ten years of living: milestones and disappointments, small successes and unfulfilled dreams.

At the end of the letter was a PS: "I was thinking about Sumanas while driving home the other night. She gets that tendency, to walk in wherever she 'smells death', from her mother. In retrospect, that was the mystery I found in you. I can remember Mom telling me that at McKinley Street, she couldn't build a fence tall enough to keep you in the yard."

Something about those PS's. So often the most potent message in the letter appears there: "Oh, by the way, I've never had the courage to tell you before, but . . ." This PS was a secret love note buried at the bottom of my sister's letter to me. Its arrow went straight to the heart.

Sanity. We are all a little timid about going into this word. We know what lurks on its other side, and none of us is exactly sure where the dark side of this moon begins. But the message of its sound might be simpler than we think.

Sanity smoothly slides in on an S; not stagnant, it flowS, it moveS. The river of s runs into an—a soft, feminine, interior place. Now the sound rises to the higher frequency of i, which vibrates between the eyebrows, the soul's lookout point, from which one can see forever.

The last syllable opens alertly with the brisk sound of t, *and then gives of itself as it ends in the energetic sound of* ee.

Yes, that sounds true: Sanity moves. It is feminine and inner. It is clear and alert. And, perhaps most importantly, it spreads itself all over the place. It is generous. It gives. Sanity.

I knew my mother felt that way—that nothing would keep me "in." My penchant for living the daring life frightened her immensely, and yet I often heard an undercurrent of respect beneath the tense voice of her reprimands. In spite of her motherly desire to protect me, something in her helplessly cheered me on.

I remember after she died, I was sitting by myself in the funeral parlor when our next-door neighbor of twenty years, Mrs. DeKing, came in. The neighbor made a point to speak briefly to each one of us children. We were the rowdy bunch she endured for a noisy eternity, but now the house would be sold and we would be leaving her life for good.

When she came to me, she looked at me tenderly and said, "There wasn't a time when your mother spoke of you that her whole face didn't light up!"

Now I wept, really wept, for the first time since my mother's passing. I had been considered one of the "black sheep" of the family, a "problem child." But now what I had always suspected was revealed: My mother delighted in my adventures on the other side of the fence. She was silently climbing with me whenever I reached for the bar on top.

For a long time now I have felt that true sanity will only be found beyond all barriers—beyond the fences we build to ward off, hold back, separate and fragment. Fences are perfect symbols of our feeble attempts to control an uncontrollable universe.

And so, this look at sanity is about the urge to climb. It is a song to the human spirit, which refuses to be fenced in, that force in us that will not call off the search until we are whole and free.

* * *

For several years I taught an adult-education course called "Sanity." The students were surprised with certificates at the last class. The presentation of the awards always brought applause and laughter. It seemed more than anyone had dared to hope for: a certificate of sanity!

I think we all are a little fearful that the crazy stowaway we are harboring on board will be discovered one day. Most students admitted lifelong fears that the skin of their sanity would at some point wear thin and the fruitcake inside would show through. As one woman put it, her sanity never felt well secured. She always worried that she might absentmindedly leave it behind, like an umbrella.

But I would like to propose this: What if our definition of sanity *included* the stowaway and the fruitcake? What if our rules were more forgiving and allowed us to lose a few umbrellas here and there? Might we not find ourselves in a refreshing if zany world? Perhaps we should all take to heart Zorba's suggestion to his boss at the end of *Zorba the Greek:* "You are a wonderful man . . . just one thing you need: a little madness."

I have been told that in Hindi there are about eight words for madness, four of which are good! These four are usually translated as some sort of Divine Madness—those wonderful crazy streaks that we all love: someone singing in the streets, someone having a heart-to-heart talk with an inanimate object, people laughing with their whole bodies. Hearts where spontaneity still reigns, minds that delight in surprise, bodies that are loose enough to allow earthquakes of sorrow and white waters of bliss to move through—souls with breathing room.

Of course, we have just described all the children of the world.

It seems we are born divinely mad—or divinely sane, if you prefer. Insanity (the kind the other four words in Hindi describe—the painful kind) is something we have to learn.

Naturally, then, it is a child who can point the way to our return. When Sumanas was five years old, we lived on Peaks

Island off the coast of Maine. On Sunday afternoons we walked around the island together. It was our time to talk.

One diamond-clear Sunday in October we took the coastal road and walked the entire circumference of the island. When we reached the wilder, less-populated northern banks, we stopped for a while to sit on the rocks and take in the spectacular view.

"Just look out there at the sea," I said to Sumanas. "See how blue it all is? Look at the royal-blue sky with the snow-white clouds blowing over it. . . . And look at the deep-blue ocean and the white, foamy surf . . ."

She gazed out at the sea and sky, deep in thought. Then she looked at me, those chocolate eyes as big as a doe's. "Yes, there's the sky above and the ocean below," she began, "but have you ever noticed how the world doesn't have any sides?"

I straightened up to look out over the ocean again and found myself suddenly transported to a world with the sides peeled away. I was surrounded by endless horizon—a spaciousness no fence could possibly mar. How did I come to take those adult-world barriers so seriously? They were so small in light of this.

As my guide and I sat together appreciating this world without end, I began to remember things from a saner time: how huge it all is, how every moment is brimming with possibility, how joy doesn't walk in single file—it dances.

No, Sumanas, I must admit, I had not noticed.

Not for a long time anyway.

T: *Trust*

꒰ꃸꋊꋬ꒱

*Do you think it's possible? Not the great
heroic act, but the little one: simply
walking hand in hand with a friend to the
next station?*

*Simply trusting one little patch of life and
letting it take you wherever it wants to
go?*

—P.P., *The Rice Washer*

"Tell me something about trust," I called into the bathroom as
my daughter stood before the mirror painstakingly perfecting
a strand of hair that curled over her temple.

"Funny you should ask," she answered, never taking her
gaze from the fascinating creature in the mirror. "Just today I
was telling a friend, 'I don't trust anybody . . .' "

DP is fifteen—sixteen in a month. She has had two major
"scenes" (boyfriends), and both, in her words, have "dissed"
her (in this case, meaning they lied).

"I was telling it to a boy who was trying to kick it to me"
(i.e., he was flirting with her). She looked at me this time as
she went on to describe the moment of truth. "I told him,
'I've stopped trusting men . . . I don't even trust my homegirls
anymore.' "

DP has taken the fall. She has bitten into the apple of experience, and the bitter taste of it lingers.

"Do you think our culture teaches distrust?" I asked.

"Heck no!" Now she came out of the bathroom and looked
at me. "Everybody *tells* you to trust . . . and you're born trusting.
You trust that the bottle will be there, and somebody'll change
your Pampers . . . it's living that teaches you not to trust."

Oh, living. She's talking about Hard Knocks. The Thief of
Innocence. Who among us has not been initiated into the world
of distrust?

The real miracle might be that trust continues. It seems to have a heart of its own. In spite of everything, trust continues.

A few days later, my own world came shattering down around me. The "new" used car I bought only a month ago had been in the shop three times, and I had just been given the mechanic's final condolences: "Dump it!" he advised.

With the wolf of financial disaster at the door, I broke in two, and a river of hopelessness flowed out. DP came home from school exactly at the moment of the flood. I poured out my tale of woe and she just smiled. "Things will work out," she said. "They always do."

I was touched for a moment as she stood there so tall and reassuring. She is indeed growing into a sensitive young woman. But still hearing the growl at my door, I went on to the question heaviest in my heart. "Things don't always work out: Thousands of people starve to death each year. People get painful diseases, people without shoes live in cardboard boxes in January," I protested.

DP held her own; there was even a glimmer of laughter in her response. "Things are going to work out. I just know it."

I saw that she was content with her sense of it as she turned and carted her books downstairs to the large basement room that is her world, but the question still hounded me. If Life is really trustworthy, how can there be so much suffering?

I know a lot of sophisticated philosophical answers to that question, from ancient Buddhist to Christian to New Age, but— in my belly and my bones—I still don't know.

Later that week, at DP's prompting, a group of teenage girls took up the question of trust again.

"You *want* to trust," the one with wild red hair said. "It might not always work out, but it feels good to trust—mad [i.e. *really, really*] good."

And that's where we left it as the group crowded around the mirror to check their hairdos and makeup before going off into another round.

A good place to leave it. Maybe the secret to trust is not

trusting because it will get you where you want to go, but simply because it feels good to trust.

Yes, I know. We are warned especially not to trust things that feel good; so often they seem to lead to our demise. And yet, what is the real treasure in life anyway? Perhaps an open heart is more valuable than anything we could possibly lose. Perhaps that's why it feels so good to trust—mad good.

Trust. Let's let the sound take us on its own journey:

Trust. A full-circle T word, beginning and ending with the sharpness of T. This might surprise you as it does me. Trust is not a limp word. There is softness at the center (us), *but that softness is carried on either end by our briskest sound.*

T: *the alphabet-mystery-school master sTrikes our desk! We jump out of our slumber, eyes growing round with wonder. Only now can the TReasure be revealed: R the golden sound of oRe, rupee and* rich. *It rewards our awakening. It reminds us of who we* Really *are: emperors disguised as beggars. Shedding the rags of poverty consciousness, we go soft. At last there is no need to defend our separate little egos:* us. Us, *the experience of connection.*

Thus awakened to our true heritage, melting into one another, once again we come upon the fresh moment: T calls us out of any new dream into which we might have slipped, invites us to begin again. And so it goes—nothing to hold on to—just one moment after another bobbing along on the river of life: Trust.

This story of trusting finds us in the age-old battlefield of gender, where war stories of betrayal abound. A good place to begin:

Terry and I ran growth groups for couples at the counseling center where I worked in the early years of our marriage. This would be our last group for a while, as I was going through a major career change: from psychologist to full-time mother. I was already learning new laws of navigation, wobbling with the extra weight of Sumanas, when we started the semester-long, weekly group.

Around the middle of the semester, Terry and I took center stage with our own issue, asking the group to help us. "I'm afraid about this change of roles," I confessed to Terry. "I've always been my own breadwinner . . . and I'm having a hard time letting go and trusting that you can hold us all up."

"I'm looking forward to holding you up," he responded, brightly at first. But soon there were tears at the rims of his eyes. "Trust me," he almost whispered. "I need you to trust me."

An activity was devised by two members of the group to dramatize what had been expressed in words: I was to close my eyes and fall backward into Terry's arms. I could not see where I was going or what he was doing behind me. It felt real enough.

I stood there pregnant and vulnerable for a few moments, then I closed my eyes and fell.

He was there, his warm hands on my back. He turned me around, fresh tears glistening in his eyes. "Trust me . . . ," he said again, and I felt a rock of ice inside me melt.

The issue was put aside as of that evening. Terry needed my trust—and I needed it. I stopped questioning his willingness or ability to hold us up. And it felt mad good to trust during those early years of child-nurturing. The world of job searches, employee reviews, promotions or demotions was far away from the farmhouse where I grew vegetables, baked bread, made fires and watched the seasons and my toddler change. After a few years, we "tried for another" and were successful in the first month.

But then when DP was less than two months old, the man who had caught me so effortlessly in the growth room was now turned in another direction: he was in love with another woman. For a while he tried to hold up two women and four children, but this created too many gaps for everyone. At last, we mutually decided for divorce.

The physical/financial tendrils were easier to untangle than the emotional fibers as we pulled apart. Sobbing one night at the deep betrayal I felt, I reminded him of that tender moment when he urged me to trust his support of my mothering.

He looked at me helplessly. "You probably shouldn't have . . . ," he admitted.

It may seem strange, but I felt true respect for Terry in that moment. He seemed so human—making vows and breaking them in spite of dazzling intentions—so much like me.

Slowly Terry and I each found our separate ways into the new lives calling us, mine drawing me closer and closer to India. Magically, by the fall of 1980, the money appeared, and the road opened for me to go.

I was living with friends in town by then, and Terry came to see me one afternoon to work out some final details of our divorce agreement. He took me outside, where we sat on the grass under a young tree.

"There's something I've been wanting to say to you for a while," he began. "You have been wanting to go deeper on the spiritual path since I met you. I have always felt that I was the one holding you back. . . ." (Once again tears of helplessness appeared at the rims of his eyes.) ". . . No matter what anybody says to you, go for it! This is where your dream is taking you—I always felt it—just give it your all. I hope it gives you everything that you long for."

We embraced for a long time under that tree; each of our faces wet with tears. I don't know how many old wounds we left composting in the grass beneath us. I lost count.

When at last Terry and I rose together, a new sense of trust rose in me. Perhaps people cannot be trusted to do what they say they will, or what we hope they will. But perhaps love is more plentiful than we ever dare believe. Perhaps it is love that is stalking us at every turn.

And love seems to be the one thing that refuses to give up on us.

U: *Understanding*

❦

The longing for truth is scattering my dreams.

—Sw. Visarjana

I once heard Elizabeth Kubler Ross, America's pioneer in death and dying, tell this story of a young girl's passing: In the months Elizabeth worked with the girl and her family, the child had grown tremendously weak and skeleton thin. Everything that could be done medically had been done; the only thing left was the dying. But the girl was unable to relax. She seemed to be caught in a turbulent struggle, using the little strength she had to fight off her death.

When Elizabeth found an opportunity to be alone with her, she said to the dying girl, "Your time has come. All you have to do now is let go. Is there something stopping you?"

The child looked up at Elizabeth through weary eyes and confided, "The nuns at school told us that people go to Heaven only if they love God more than anybody else. . . . And I love my mommy and daddy more. . . ."

There must have been a grave silence in that room as this crippling interpretation of divine love found its way to Elizabeth's understanding heart. "Loving your mommy and daddy is a way of loving God," she said at last. "God has no arms to put around you, no hands to put on your forehead. He cannot tell stories that make you laugh; he cannot bring you a stuffed monkey. So he uses your mommy and daddy for these things. Every time you feel love for your mommy and daddy, you are loving God."

The girl visibly relaxed then. The message must have resonated with her own experience of loving; it was something she could understand . . . and in the night she peacefully passed.

Understanding. What does this sound provoke in us?

We have two words standing together, like two Chinese calligraphy characters sharing a roof. Let's take them one by one:

Under. *We begin with the sound of ignorance:* uh. *Perhaps all understanding begins here:* uh . . . *And the natural response to ignorance is to go* iNside: N. *Our attention within, we move into* der. *Beginning with the driving, daring, doing sound of* d *and rhyming with stir, we are drowned in the pot. We are* Under.

Now, at the root of things, we Stand.

Stand. *We rise from the ocean floor with the graceful movement of* S. *Refreshed from our journey, our attention is easily focused with the sharp sound of* t. *And because we have plumbed the depths, there is nothing left to fear or fight. We soften:* an.

Our word ends with d, *that strong, ready-for-action sound. We have mined the strength that arises from softness. The sound has given us a map: Understanding begins with admitting our ignorance which leads us beneath the surface where we find the strength not only to stand, but to live. Not merely to live, but to live in tenderness:* Understand.

Someone once asked my meditation master Osho why we never seem able to live according to what we understand. The usual answer to this familiar quandary is that we are not sufficiently committed to our understanding. Essentially we are weak willed. Lazy.

But Osho's answer, as I remember it, was something like this: You must be fooling yourself, thinking you understand. You must have borrowed someone else's ideas and called it understanding. When you really come to an understanding, your behavior changes in accordance with it. Understanding is always transformative.

Although this answer reassures us that we don't have to beat ourselves into submission, it takes some courage to swallow its medicine. For it exposes most of our ''understandings'' as false and useless. We will have to ''unhitch the universe,'' as a

Zen poet once advised. We will have to learn to walk more lightly, with less gravitational pull.

And there is no need to be confused; the acid test is simple. Anything we are holding we can let go. Anything we feel the weight of, anything we *stoop* under, is not our under*stand*ing.

This miracle is an insight brought back from a flight into the dreaming mind: For the year following his death, my father frequently appeared in my dreams. In all the dreams he was young, healthy and alert, showing no scars from his recent battles with cancer, chemotherapy and radiation treatments. As is usual in dreams, I took his healthy condition for granted. But in one particular dream I remembered that he had, in reality, died.

A shock wave surged through me as I stood there facing the man who had been my father, realizing that he was no longer of this world. But the initial rush of fear soon melted as I took in the relaxed, loving presence before me.

For a timeless moment we stood silently together, savoring the rare circumstance. We were standing on the borderline between two universes.

He knows the Other World, I thought. He can tell me about it.

Now a new fear rose in me: Dare I ask about his passage? Would I have the strength to withstand his answer? I was so close to the line already, perhaps I would fall in.

But the opportunity was too extraordinary to miss. I took courage and leapt:

"Tell me what it's like on the other side," I nearly whispered.

He looked at me with great tenderness and opened his mouth to speak. This is what I heard:

"Gnneet scummm krat un lockern bluum . . . schutip glubbern ta scarlish krat . . ."

I strained to hear him. He caught the disappointment in my eyes and strained to speak more clearly:

"Do libernica ash zeet curna mana cue . . ."

I tried harder; he turned up the volume:

"Da libernica ash zeet curna mana cue!!"

We gazed at each other in utter helplessness. The intensity of the moment woke me up.

I looked about my dark room.

I was back on this shore. My father and every hint of the other world had vanished.

For a while, I sat alone in the night and tried again to decipher what my father was trying to tell me. But slowly I sank into a disappointed sleep.

I carried the dream's disturbing puzzle with me throughout the day until its message bled through the other-worldly language that seemed to be all my father now knew: It's no use getting ahead of ourselves. Understanding grows out of living fully, right where we are. It comes through intimate contact with our own lives, and that is its grace.

Perhaps Henry David Thoreau expressed it most eloquently when, on his deathbed he was asked what the other world was like.

It is said that he answered, "One world at a time...."

V: Vision

꧁꧂

*The secret to seeing innocently is to see from
a new viewpoint, one that is not conditioned by
what you expect to see.*

*If you could really see that tree over there
. . . you would be so astounded that you'd
fall over.*

—Deepak Chopra, *The Way of the Wizard*

A friend of mine used to run an avant-garde photography school. He had studied with Ansel Adams and was himself a much sought-after teacher, known for his uniquely unusual approach to the art form. One of his favorite teaching methods was requiring his students to shoot a roll of film blindfolded.

When I first heard this, I laughed. I took it for one of those delightfully ridiculous games born of the 1960s—pure experiments in freedom. But for many years now, whenever I am in the woods, my mind turns to that assignment.

Sometimes I stand with my eyes closed—feeling the wind and the sun, smelling the air—and I find myself magnetically pulled toward some direction. It seems there is a sense organ in my belly which knows how to see without eyes.

Vision. Make the first sound and behold: v-v-v. We are entering the Upper Stratosphere of the alphabet. We have arrived at the Vibrational plane. We are on higher ground.

And so, vibrating at the leVel of a bird's eye view, we open to our vowel: the short I. I brings us into the third eye, the sixth chakra of the human energy system where clear vision (both inner and outer) is possible. We enter the realm of seeing what is, rather than what we hope or fear might be.

In this first syllable, we have arrived at a viewing place and the eye with which to see. What does the second half of the word bring?

This version of S—si—is also vibrationally vibrant. We leap from the third eye into the mouth, and rattle our sounding instruments— lips, tongue and teeth—like a shaman's gourd. We chase away any beast that might stand in our way; we embrace the courage to see.

Having bravely faced the Mountain of the Here and Now, we soften and return to the Experiencer: ion, a soft drone of a sound, briefly touching again on i, and then sliding deeper inside (on) as the ears close out any sound but the inner silence.

All teachings in some way blind us. We must courageously shake ourselves up and then sit alone at the center if we are to see. Vision.

In one of the meditation classes I taught at Cornell, a particularly shy student spoke only once about the effect meditation had on him. After an hour in one of the university courtyards doing *vipassana* (sitting silently and watching the breath) and a Zen walk (a very slow walk, paying full attention to the experience of walking), he approached me and said:

"Everything looks different after I've been sitting for a while. The most ordinary thing—like someone opening a window— becomes so beautiful. . . ."

This is what I call Vision.

I don't know exactly why, but it seems a universal goal of enculturation to render us blind. Unfortunately, we don't usually realize this blindness until our vision is regained. And that often takes a miracle. Here is a small example:

When I was in graduate school I took a drawing class that met in the evenings on the far end of campus. The teacher wanted us to learn the skill of reproducing, as faithfully as possible, whatever he put before us. For weeks we practiced bringing to paper, with only a pencil, the sleekness of glass, the intricate textures of wood, the soft, curving peaks and valleys of draped cloth.

I became so easily lost in these objects that I was usually stunned when the three-hour session was over. But the real surprise was pulling back from my paper and finding there a shiny stemmed glass filled with water, a wooden box in the shadowed background, and a velvety piece of cloth, which begged to be touched.

Once the teacher leaned over my shoulder at the end of a session and looked into my paper. "Ever think you could do that?" he asked.

It was a hard question to answer because I was certain that it wasn't I who had done it. The process is difficult to describe, though I have heard many artists try: It is not the cold matter of eye-hand coordination that brings objects to life on a piece of paper. It is intimacy. I did not trace the lines of that cloth, I wrapped myself in it. I lost myself in its rolling hills and surrendered my boundaries; I *became* that cloth.

The picture was a by-product of this intimacy—a surprise bonus. And there was yet another bonus, equally surprising:

As I left the class one evening and walked out into a spring night, I found myself in a strange new world. I was not looking through my eyes in the normal shallow way, but from a place deeper inside my body. While drawing, I must have fallen from my labeling mind and dropped into my belly. Walking through the world at a gut level, I reclaimed a pair of innocent eyes through which everything became more and more profoundly three-dimensional. It was as though I had lived my entire life on a cardboard set and was seeing depth for the first time.

I walked in awe through the inner campus with its big old trees, which were now mysterious creatures—huge and round—vibrating with life. I, myself, was a citizen of this three-dimensional world—another of its creatures—round and whole and intensely alive.

This is our predicament. If we render our world flat, we ourselves become cardboard. If we draw borders around ourselves, everything in our world gets imprisoned with us. But if the boundaries between us and just one small thing are erased—if we enter it and allow it to enter us—then the whole planet is freed.

And what will we see if we permanently erase the lines we have imposed over our world? We'll see a festival of lights out there—a world full of dancing creatures . . . a party!

All we need to do is let one small detail overwhelm us, drop into our bellies and feel a little deeper. Open our eyes and *see*.

W: *Windows*

୧୨୧୨

*Everything looks different after I've been
sitting for a while. The most ordinary thing—
like someone opening a window—becomes so
beautiful.*

—Cornell University Meditation Student

I could have just as easily chosen "words" for this chapter's topic. I spend a lot of time in wonder over them—those colorful beads that roll off my tongue or slip through my fingers as I string together a tale. Then I would have talked about the Mystery of Speech: All those words coming up out of nowhere, weaving together stories, random thoughts, and eavesdroppings.

Of course, I would have also had to talk about the impotence of words as I remembered times when death touched me, when beauty or love high-jacked me and brought me to the secret place where words are too big and boisterous to enter.

Or I could have picked "women." And then I would have told you about Priya's devastating honesty. You might have wondered with me why her reputation (even with herself) is that she is too judgmental, when all I hear when I am around her is one nearly unbearable note of compassion.

I might have told you about Abhishek's way of closing her eyes when she is about to share her strongest feelings, how her fingers dance when she speaks. You would have seen tears spring to her eyes in unexpected moments, and you might have caught some of her contagious, unbridled laughter as it burst through her careful New England seams.

Surely I would have told you about Alicia's outrageously irreverent reverence for life. And about Mary's insatiable thirst to touch and be touched; how she took over the strolling minstrel's guitar in Mexico, singing *"Des Colores"* to forty wet pairs of eyes, the wettest belonging to the minstrel himself.

And about Carol, who ran barefoot in the Maine snow for her mail, who could stretch dinner-for-two to dinner-for-a-dozen, storytelling all the while, whose eyes were portholes to a silent sea of feeling. And Betsy, who never forgot how to laugh, even as the bone cancer was eating her inside-out. And Shari, who would drop anything to go walking with a friend, anytime of day or night. And Veet, who saw the cosmic drama unfolding in her compost bin. And Nartana whose X-ray vision could always spot the truth trying to get out through a fence of words.

I would have had to speak of my saucy grandmother, my unpretentious mother, the blossoming of my daughters. It would have been a long chapter. . . .

Then again . . . I might have chosen "watching," "witnessing," or "waiting," any of the many meditative flowers one can gather from the sunlit peaks of the mountainous, high-altitude letter of *W*.

But I didn't. I chose "windows"—the common openings between worlds where winds and ideas pass, where light, sound, fragrance and possibility enter: Windows.

Let's lend our ear to this everyday word and let it open our mind.
Windows. The key word hidden within windows is, of course, wind. *Close your eyes and whisper the sound a few times:* wind, wind, wind. . . . *Feel the breeze of it. Feel the lips puckering up and then being blown all the way back:* wind.

To open with W *sets the stage for* wonder. *Without* W *we would have difficulty speaking of* wandering, *wilderness or wonders of the world.* How would we talk of waves *or* water *or* wombs? *Without* W, *perhaps we could never truly understand* wickedness *or* wounds.

W *is a wind, in and of itself.* In *takes the unruly, mysterious experience of wind* INside, *and* d, *a definite sound of determination, stands poised for action.*

But the only action necessary when one stands before a window is opening: o . . . oh . . . [ow]. *The final* W *is silent. Perhaps, now that we have opened the window to ourselves, this final W is added to bring us full circle—back to the wind.*

The deepest experience of the ordinary always takes us full circle. Once a Zen master described his experience like this: "Before I was enlightened, mountains were mountains, and rivers were rivers. Then I meditated for many years, and mountains were no longer mountains, and rivers were no longer rivers. But now I have finally awakened, and once again mountains are mountains, and rivers are rivers."

Meditate upon a window and it may open a new world to you, a world beyond your small personal life and its troubles. In the end, of course, you will return to your familiar world with its floors, walls and windows. But there will be one small difference: the wind will be in your heart—sweeping away the dust as it gathers, lifting the kite of your dreams. Try it today: Windows.

The wheel (interestingly enough, another *W* word) always takes the honors as man's greatest invention. But, I ask you, what was life without the window? At first, when we lived in the trees, the window was a moot point, of course—our home being space itself. But once the first wall was up, the invention of the window could not have been far behind.

Just think of that first breath of fresh air—the opening. In my version of how it all must have happened, the most heartfelt prayer of thanks was not said over a meal, but gazing through a window.

Windows are the constant reminders of a greater world beyond our own house, ushering in its fragrances, colors, moods and sounds. Every window provides such a steady stream of miracles that they are taken for granted and easy to miss. But if you station yourself for, say, weeks on end in front of a window, you just might be struck by a stray miracle. I happened to be lucky enough once to have such a station in life:

As part of my life in a spiritual commune, I worked as a cook in a vegetarian restaurant whose clientele, in the first year of business, was limited to a few loyal regulars. That meant large, idle gaps in the life of the cook. About midday, after making the Soup du Jour, the Day's Crêpe and the Chinese Special; after the midmorning omelet rush; after the little lunch crowd went back to their offices, I would while away the hours at the take-out window.

Though we did offer tofu hot dogs and French fries through that window, no one seemed to know it, and no one ever came to order anything. It was a large picture window, which looked out onto the street of what might be called a fringe neighborhood—between the upscale, polished-glass businesses and the boarded-up graffiti part of town.

I watched citizens of all worlds pass by that window. And, simultaneously, I witnessed my heartstrings get plucked, tugged and sometimes frozen by the dramas that played themselves out, unaware of my watching.

Young couples walked by giggling and stroking one another; oblivious to everything around them. Old couples tiredly limped by, their faces falling with gravity, oblivious to each other. Women went by with squalling babies crumpled up in portable strollers; men with no legs went by in wheelchairs.

People stopped on the street corner to shout at one another, kiss, or look into the trees in the little green across the way. Women in colorful clothing took hurried small steps as they passed by, giggling and gossiping with one another. Skinheads wove their way on skateboards through the masses. Small groups of people strode together in perfect unison, looking like multiheaded, multilimbed creatures.

People carried vegetables, briefcases and musical instruments. Children carried tattered dolls, ice-cream cones and helium balloons.

Sometimes it was dark and rainy, and everyone hunched under umbrellas or newspapers. Sometimes it was sunny and bright, and people came out in brimmed hats and sunglasses. Sometimes it was cold and windy, and almost no one came.

Once in a while an ambulance or fire truck, ablaze with whirling red lights, screamed through the streets.

Every part of my own being emerged, passed through me like a storm, and disappeared again.

There was no time to cling to any single image. My consciousness was a mirror that the world danced before. Or was the window *my* mirror, reflecting back to me my youth and my age, my conservative streak and my adolescent rebellion, my dark side and my light, my hopes and my fears?

All I know is that after several weeks of sitting by the window, I was able to watch the inner parade with more detachment. Sometimes I could even enjoy a private mind-drama full of pathos—accompanied by the big-band sound of my heart-strings—without taking sides.

It's all a marvel. Both inside and out. This is what I learned from the tofu-hot-dog take-out window that nobody visited.

Because windows are perfect vehicles for the meditative spirit, the lessons that blow through them are endless. If I were to express my gratitude to all the windows that have created openings in my mind, this chapter could be almost as long as the "women" chapter I decided not to write. But I cannot leave the world of windows until I thank one more. This window did not show me pictures, it spoke:

While I was working in the communally run restaurant, I lived in our communally run hotel. It was the only time in my life that I lived in a large city, and when my window was open on a summer evening, the chaos of sound pouring through was astounding to me: a myriad of traffic noises, alarms, people shouting. . . .

I worked long shifts at the restaurant, often twelve hours. When I arrived home at the end of my workday, I was always exhausted, but sometimes I had gone over the hump and entered a state that can only be called *deliciously tired.* I was in such a state on the night my bedroom window spoke to me.

My body was buzzing with the intensity of a full day when I stumbled into the room and flopped onto my bed. I gave my aching muscles over to the mattress, while I lay there, wide awake, supersensitive to my surroundings.

The room was dark except for an orange neon glow from the gas station across the street. The air around me was hot and humid, my skin damp with perspiration. The open window over my bed provided an occasional welcome breeze.

In this relaxed state, I fell into a place deep inside myself, a place from which the clamor of the city seemed far away. I could listen to the riotous urban roar as though it were a chorus of cicadas.

Suddenly from this lulling ocean of sound emerged a gigantic cheer: "Yeeaaa! Yeeaaa!"

Then all was silent.

Moments later a different but equally loud cheer breached the stillness like a mammoth whale: "Boooo! Boooo!"

And the silence was richer than before.

Now the silence was punctuated by a muffled human voice coming over a PA system. I was hearing a summer-evening baseball game at the local stadium, and it continued this way for most of an hour: "Yeeaaa! Yeeaaa!"—silence—"Yeeaaa!"—silence—"Boooooooo!"

Unable to move from my position of alert collapse, I listened for a long while until a chuckle came over me: Why, that's an echo of my own mind I'm hearing: Judging all the events as they play through my life—constantly yeaing and booing. I suddenly saw the ridiculous arrogance of it, the folly of sitting on the sidelines of my own life, keeping score when I could simply be out there enjoying the play.

Novelist Tom Robbins once noted that we are all constantly involved in chanting the only two great mantras that have ever existed: yum and yuk . . . with the one possible exception, he eventually added: Yipes!

(He must have had the window open.)

X: *X*

*To be or
not to be,
that is the question.*

— Shakespeare,
Hamlet

Foreboding and mysterious *X:* Feel the stark finality in this single sweep of a word; notice her uncanny ability to stand alone in a crowd, self-sufficient and free.

Chameleonic *X* moves through language taking on many forms. She gives an enigmatic air to anyone who walks with her: Madam X, Malcom X, Planet X, Generation X. She is the mathematician of the transcendental; speaking of X amount of dollars or the X number of people it would take to bring peace to the planet. Only *X* has shown the courage to lend herself to all the *e*X-husbands, *e*X-wives and *e*X-lovers of the world. Perhaps her presence is what has softened us to this growing substrata of the population, as we each learn to speak tenderly of our ex.

But *X*'s greatest mystery is that she can stand for any one of us. If we are unable to write our name, we can merely make an *X* on the dotted line. Without any of the frills of personality, that *X* marks the spot of a human, purely being. Like the *X*'s on the maps in the state parks, or at the mall announcing, "You are here," this *X* on the dotted line affirms, "I am here. Right here at the point where two possibilities cross."

Such is the human predicament: We are the collision point of duality, a continual crossroads of possibilities. Whatever drama is being played out around us, we are forever gazing into the face of one choice: to be or not to be.

The *X* on the dotted line reflects a moment of truth. For this moment, at least, one has chosen to be. One has looked deeply into the treasure map and found the spot where the treasure is hidden—You are here: *X*.

X is mysterious even in her sound-making. When X begins a word—xylophone, xenophobia, Xanthippe—*she almost always becomes a mocking bird, borrowing Z's song. But when X is safe inside a word, she cries out—we hear her in the sharp sound of an* ax, *the disconcerting bootheels of the* taxman *(and other* taxing *situations), the satisfying sound of a lid fitting its* box. X *is particularly good at endings.*

When X stands alone, we hear ourselves say, eks. *Coming from inside an old familiar rut, we helplessly utter,* e. *But out of this low, we suddenly leap into our full energy:* ks!—*a powerful, gutsy sound. I am here, where the past has been X-ed, and the future is open. I am here, a convergence of divergent paths, as mysterious to myself as I am to you: X!*

Many crossroads have brought me to the place I am now. I have come this way through many decisions to Be. Of course, just as often I have given into temptations Not to Be, to slide back into sleep. It takes so much courage to live, it is almost unbelievable.

I choose this story about finding the courage to Be because my little cry of *e* was so helpless, and the resulting *ks* was so, well, miraculous:

It was a cold winter in a little town in the Catskill Mountains of New York. I was working several low-paying jobs at the time, but had recently lost the one that paid the rent. This was particularly disastrous as my daughters Sumanas and DP were older now—teen and preteen respectively—with bigger bodies to clothe and bigger mouths to feed, not to mention their discovery of such necessities as nail polish, hair ornaments, and brand-name sneakers.

My mind was constantly mulling over new enterprises that might keep the three of us afloat. I rewrote my resume a dozen times, applying for any job that smelled, even remotely, like my cup of tea. I considered the full gamut of small businesses that I had, admittedly with very little success, attempted before. But as the debts piled up, and no new source of income manifested, things began to look pretty grim.

In such a dark atmosphere, all the stresses of single parenthood beyond the financial arena flourished like mushrooms in a cave. A good example of mushrooms-gone-wild was our weekly laundry trip. The nearest Laundromat was half an hour's drive away, but the long pilgrimage was only the beginning. Sumanas—treading the murky waters of puberty—had rightly earned her reputation as Queen of Chaos: clean clothes and dirty were wrapped around each other all over the bedroom floor, as if there had been some mythological battle in the night between the soiled and the renewed, neither ever winning. This, along with DP's fickle nature compelling her to change outfits every few hours, resulted in six or more loads of laundry per week, which had to be lugged down the thirty-six steps from our apartment, up Sled Hill (aptly named), to the car. Then it would be driven for half an hour, accompanied by deafening rap music played on the tape deck (with intermittent arguing about the choice and volume of music), stuffed into washers, schlepped into dryers, folded and stacked into mountains (which I painfully remember on more than one occasion toppling onto the dirty, wet floor).

In the midst of this monumental task were homework assignments with their inevitable lost or dirtied papers, arguments between the sisters, and—now that we were in the "big city" of Kingston, New York—a bad case of The Wants. The mall was just over the hill, with all its glitz, marked-down bins, and "fly" (interesting) boys. And if persuasions failed to move me up the hill, there was always the food store around the corner or the vending machines right there in Suds Your Duds.

I never looked forward to this ritual cleansing. Well, maybe once, when we combined it with buying DP's first formal evening dress for the sixth-grade dance, but all other Tuesday nights carried the added weight of my darkest dread.

This particular Tuesday night, the dread did not lift even as we placed the square mountains of clean clothes into the baskets, loaded the car, drove on slippery roads through the snow, and dragged all six bins down Sled Hill and up the thirty-six steps home. Another trial-by-laundry was only a week away.

As I dropped the last bin on the living-room floor and let go my heaviest sigh, I noticed the flashing red light on my answering machine: word from the planet's surface!

My sister-in-law Monette's voice was on the machine, leaving one of a series of relayed messages from a former college beau who had been trying to reach me, through her, for several weeks.

Here was an obvious crossroads. Someone is knocking at my door, and I'm going to open it and have a look, I thought. I signed my X on the dotted line and, springing from this dismal moment, committing myself "to Be," I lifted the phone from the receiver and dialed Michael's number in Ithaca, New York.

On the phone was the voice of an intimate stranger—one whose *Loounggg* Island accent I knew, literally, by heart, but whom I had left behind many lifetimes ago. We talked about marriages and careers, successes and failures. He had found Osho on his own and was reading his books, and that made me happy.

The laughter came as easily as it had in the backseat of his white Mustang. Would I let him come to visit? Of course—next week, Monday night, before the next great pilgrimage to Suds Your Duds.

Michael was not the man I had imagined him to grow into when we parted ways in college. The fast-talking, dark-eyed champion swimmer was much softer around the edges than I could have foreseen. We eyed each other cautiously yet gently through faces that time and gravity had transformed. Then he presented me with a bouquet of flowers he had kept hidden behind his back. I put them in a vase and we had tea.

The day was wet and windy, so we decided to take his pickup to get DP from the middle school instead of letting her walk. Something in the way that he climbed into the cab revealed to me the untouched eighteen-year-old boy who was still alive and well in there. The rest was easy.

He came with me to the meditation and yoga classes that I taught that night. And the next night . . . he helped fold laundry!

Before he left to return to Ithaca on Wednesday, we took a walk in the woods.

"I don't want this to be just one of those 'Oh that was nice and interesting' things. I want us to continue and see where we can go together," he hazarded.

"We'll see . . . ," I replied, staying reserved.

"I want you to move to Ithaca!" he blurted out. His dreams were flying at *hyperspace speed now.* "I think I can get you a job at Cornell teaching yoga and meditation. . . . They teach courses like that there, and you're good at teaching; you're really good."

"Great idea," I laughed as I put my arm around the eighteen-year-old incurable dreamer's waist.

A few weeks, and a few visits, later, Michael was on the telephone. "I have a name you should call at Cornell. He's the director of the Physical Education Department and he said he'd like to talk to you."

I took down the number and called it the next day.

"Al Gantert," the voice on the other end introduced himself, "what can I do for you?"

I told him that I was a certified yoga and meditation teacher, but before I could get very far into my presentation, Al interrupted me saying, "I already have several excellent yoga teachers, but I'm very interested in someone who can teach a course in meditation. When can you come in?"

I had already planned my first visit to Michael's cabin in Ithaca for that weekend, so an interview with Al was set for Monday morning.

Friends who knew better than I of Cornell's straight-laced reputation, urged me to dress conservatively for the interview. ". . . And keep away from topics like palmistry and psychic phenomena," they warned. I put on an anonymous white cotton top and pants, but I couldn't resist wearing my Birkenstocks and a rainbow scarf.

Al brought me into the office and closed the door. He opened the conversation by talking about the challenges of single parenthood and about the challenges of life in general. His parents had both died within the span of a year as mine had; his divorce followed on the heels of those deaths as did mine. All this had opened his heart and mind in the same way my heart had been opened.

Eventually our conversation turned to meditation: "This year, too many kids jumped off the bridges here," Al began, "so I got to thinking, 'What do these kids need that we are not giving them?' and then it came to me, 'Meditation! We need to offer these kids meditation. . . .'

"The way I live, I don't do much . . . Most of the time I just notice what is needed and wait. . . ." Now he gestured to me and said, "So I see that Life has brought me my meditation teacher. Welcome."

After that I read Al's palms and we talked about dreams, visions, and the witnessing space of meditation. We closed our meeting with a plan for me to submit a course-proposal. When I left my new friend's office, my jaw was still open.

These moments always come as a surprise to me. I constantly worry that we come into this world with a preordained quota of miracles and surely, by now, I have used mine up. But somehow it goes on. Like in my favorite circus act, delightful, ridiculous clowns keep jumping out of the tiny car.

Sometimes two of these clowns meet and dance together. Al felt the appearance of his meditation teacher to be as much a miracle as my finding the job I loved. It seems every once in a while my miracle—tiptoeing beneath her striped, fringed umbrella—and your miracle—in his big polka-dot bow tie— are such a perfect match that they'll skip off hand in hand under the Big Top.

Y: *Yes*

"Yes" is the goddam axis on which the universe turns.

—Swami Bodhi Raghu, a modern whirling dervish

I don't know how to tie a necktie. I did know once, but I forgot. Being a woman, this has not been a skill I needed to keep polished. But for some of you, it has been as essential as brushing your teeth. You could tie a tie in your sleep.

The story of a friend begins here: half alseep at the morning ritual of tying his tie. He stands before the mirror, watching his hands guide the knot up toward his Adam's apple, but the knot never makes it. About halfway up the friend begins to sob. He just can't go on like this, cutting his life off at the throat every morning.

At first his wife is sympathetic, but when the sobs continue over breakfast, she starts to worry. And when, still in tears, he calls his supervisor in the garment district, where our friend has made a name for himself in sales over the last fifteen years, and tells him that he isn't coming in today, the wife's concern takes a serious turn.

In the late morning, after the man with no knot at his throat cries a river that runs from the kitchen right through the living room, the wife takes him to a psychiatrist.

The psychiatrist asks the usual questions, to which our friend responds with tears, tears and more tears. He is unable to express anything but tears. The psychiatrist gives him a prescription for depression medication and sends him home.

The wife begs her husband to take the pills, but he refuses.

He keeps on crying. At last he dries himself off enough to get into the car and head north for Bear Mountain.

He wanders around on top of the mountain until he is alone, deep in the woods and, from there, with the faucets of his heart still running full blast, he prays.

"I can't go on," he tells the Benevolent Ear in the Sky, "so I let go of it all. Right here. Right now. Take whatever you want: My job, my house, my wife, my child—everything I've been holding onto so tightly. Take whatever you need; just bring a little peace to my heart."

As he returns from the mountain, our friend's tears gradually diminish to the sparse patterings of a dying thunderstorm. A small ray of peace finds its way through the gray clouds now dispersing in his heart.

As it turns out, in very short order our friend loses everything: the job, the house, the wife and the daughter. He learns to hang wallpaper and never wears a tie. I have heard you can't find a seam anywhere in his work. Just walking into one of his newly papered rooms, a little peace dawns.

Sometimes trying to be positive, we get confused and think it means pleasing others. But very often what looks like a "No" through everybody else's eyes is really a "Yes" to ourselves.

That "Yes" often leads to a long wild ride . . . but isn't that what we're here for, after all?

Yes—such a soft, yearning *sound. Meant to be whispered, Yes is the sound a heart makes as it opens.*

Often we fear the open skies of Yes. We have planted our roots in the dark rocky soil of No and feel safe there. No keeps things small and predictable. Yes takes us to God knows where.

Fittingly, Yes begins with expansive, branching Y—making that yearning *sound from deep in the throat where our longings gather, waiting to be sung. The sound of y acknowledges this wistful gathering and gives it voice.*

The short e that follows sings of our helplessness, bundles of human longing that we are. And the s empties our hot-air bag—we let go of judgment, we relax, we melt. . . . And so Yes is the proverbial short-but-sweet story: Singing our longings, singing our helplessness, we dissolve in surrender.

*What was all that armor of No supposed to do for us anyway?
Standing naked, the sun is so warm: Yes.*

As James Joyce's 644-page opus, ULYSSES, reaches its last page, it is slowly consumed by an insistent, irrepressible Yes. We are allowed entry into the stream of a young woman's thoughts as they crescendo and dissolve into silence. Memories of the moment she opened herself to her lover flood her mind and the remembrance melts her heart once again. The music of her Yes is, at first, slow and melodic—a single Yes arising with each thought. But soon Yes has a life of its own, arising in mid-sentence, leaving thoughts in mid-air. The rhythm becomes wilder until Yes arises with each breath. When she is burning with Yes, her logical mind is consumed in its flames and she is released: ". . . and yes I said yes I will Yes."

"Yes" is perhaps the sexiest word in the English language. It is the implosion of passion, the feminine principle of endless opening. To enter "Yes" is to free-fall through the mind and heart, and then to disappear.

Any sincere discussion of the sweet surrender of "Yes" will find us roaming the outskirts of sexual experience. It is in this sacred intimacy that most of us have tasted our first spontaneous "Yes." I have suspected for a long time that this is the real magnetism of sex. Far more potent than biological drive is the visit, however brief, to the oasis of Trust. Perhaps this is why we have such difficulty suppressing our sexual longings, and why we ought not even try. Let the seed of loving, trusting sex sprout and spread the Sacred Yes far and wide in our lives.

This is my tale of yes:

One bright Saturday in August, in a little garden outside the small coastal town of Robinhood, Maine, I was picking beans with Adityo—squatting opposite him as we poked through the foliage, looking for treasure. A gap came in our conversation and I was swallowed up in the mind's whirlpool of endless questions.

Finally I looked up over the bean bush and asked, "Do I have a choice?"

Adityo's face lit up and he let go a laugh. "Of course!" he

exclaimed. "Of course you have a choice; you *always* have a choice. . . ."

He twinkled at me from beneath his straw hat and paused just long enough for a receptive space to open in me: "It's no."

What a mysterious answer. If "No" was the only choice, what choice was that? What happened to "Yes"? And yet, Adityo's response rang true. If we remain choiceless as we float along on the river of life, the current will take us wherever it is going. We can relax. Choice is only relevant when we want to resist the current, when we want to swim upstream or step out of the flow. Choice is only relevant when we want to say "No."

Our conversation had actually started the night before, when I walked into the retreat center Adityo ran. After a warm hug, he fired at me, point-blank: "So, when are you going to India?"

"I can't go to India!" I blurted out forcefully; he had caught me in what I thought was my most private dream. "I have two little kids and no money. There is no way I can go to India."

His eyes softened as he looked into me again and said, "The kids might make it difficult, but the money isn't a problem. Money is never a problem."

He was unmoved as I described my situation: no income, no savings, no collateral; my hands virtually tied with caring for two very small children.

"You get clear that where you need to be is India, and the money will be there tomorrow," was all he would say.

Naturally I wanted to believe him, but how could I? This was not the economics I had lived by for thirty-some years. My mind was full of practical questions: Where would the money come from? How could it happen so quickly? And the most important question of all: What if I got clear that I needed to be in India, and the money didn't come? Isn't that a good definition of Hell: feeling with all your heart that you need to be somewhere and having no way to get there?

Getting clear was risky business. I wasn't sure that I wanted to know what I needed.

But that evening I had gone into the meditation, and today I had been swept away by the beauty of the retreat center and the people working and visiting there. My inner voice seemed to be saying more and more clearly that I must go and meet Osho—the Indian mystic I had encountered first through his books, then through his unconventional and expressive meditation techniques, and now through the inspired people at this meditation center—but the intense passion of that newfound voice was frightening. I wondered if I even had a choice in the matter.

A few hours after picking the beans and eating them for lunch, several of us were on Adityo's sailboat splashing atop the clear blue waters of a remote bay. There had been some singing, storytelling and wine, and now we had all fallen silent, soaking up the day's radiance. I was leaning back, losing myself in the clouds, when someone shouted, "Omigod! We have a visitor—look starboard!"

I stood up to lean over the boat and found myself face-to-face with a seal whose eyes seemed to hold as much wonder as I felt in my own. Overflowing my brim, I began to laugh and cry at once while those huge dark eyes continued to melt me into a larger and larger puddle. Then he vanished back into his watery world.

Dizzy with delight, I fell back into my seat, where I wept and laughed some more. And out of this bubbling pot of glee, a prayer formed itself inside me. A prayer of gratitude with "Yes" at its center:

"Okay, Whoever is running this ship, the world you have given me so far has been more magical than I ever could have imagined. If You want to take me to India, I'll go . . . just make it clear, really clear, that this is where I'm to go next. I need a sign—especially because of the children . . ."

After the sailboat ride, I left the meditation center and went to pick up my daughters, who spent the weekend with their father. He was living in the house we owned together that we had put up for sale a few weeks before. When I had left the kids for the weekend, Terry mentioned that an elderly couple was coming to look at the house on Saturday. In the not-so-far back of my mind, I was hoping that the couple had made an offer, and this might be how the money to go to India would manifest.

But when I arrived at the house, Terry told me that the couple never showed, and that nobody else had responded to the ad. My heart sank a bit, but was soon elevated by lively interchange with my two rambunctious traveling companions. I took them home and put them to bed, still feeling rejuvenated by the day in the sun and my interlude with the seal.

Moments later, the phone rang. It was Terry, whom I had just seen an hour ago.

He wasted no time getting down to business. "I just wanted to know," he began, "if I gave you $8,000 for your part of the house tomorrow, would you take it?"

Tomorrow reverberated in my head as I struggled to keep hold of the phone, which suddenly felt like a ton of bricks in my hand. "Tomorrow?" I asked, my jaw still open. The offer seemed impossible. Terry was barely squeaking by on his monthly check and he had no savings. "Where would you get the money to buy me out tomorrow?"

It seems his girlfriend had sold her house that week and was looking to reinvest her money. "It's in the bank and she is willing to buy you out tomorrow, if you agree to this price and we can make the trade clean and easy."

I told Terry I would have to think about it, which was essentially a lie. My mind's think-function had spun out. But I did need a little time to absorb the magnitude of the sign. I hung up the phone and murmured out loud, "It looks like I'm going to India."

Now eight thousand dollars does not sound like a lot of money for half of a house, I know. And, even though this was many years ago when eight thousand dollars was a lot more, it was not a great deal from my side. Still, the fact remained that more than enough money had flown to me on the wind of my prayer, and once I said "Yes" to this offer, the details of my journey fell effortlessly into place like a flock of geese coming in for a landing on a calm lake.

In two weeks, my divorce complete, the children staying

with Terry and his girlfriend in the house I no longer owned, I was boarding a plane to India.

On the flight from Frankfurt to Bombay, I befriended a vivacious German woman, who had been living outside the ashram where I was going. She had planned on returning to India with her mother, but the elderly woman had fallen ill.

And so I was offered the extra inland plane ticket and the room in my new friend's house, which had been prepared for her mother. When we arrived at the house, I was welcomed by a housemate with a wreath of flowers over my head and led through hallways of marble to a room overlooking the garden.

I have always been intrigued by the potlatches of Native American Tribes of the Northwest. These ceremonial feasts were tournaments of generosity, where each gift-giver tried to outdo the previous gift. It seems I was engaged in a kind of potlatch with Existence. Every "Yes" on my part was met by a more enthusiastic and lavish "Yes" from the world.

Do we have a choice in this potlatch? Of course. We are always free; we can always say "No."

But Existence would be so disappointed.

Z: Zen stick

*The fundamental of the Zen approach is that
all is as it should be, nothing is missing.
This very moment everything is perfect.*

—Osho, *The Goose is Out*

At Zen's gate one doffs the garments of dogma, belief and
cultivated virtue. All travel naked here—in this—the most mysterious of mystery schools. For it is only when we are caught
off guard that the thing might happen.

What thing is that? We might slip out of illusion and enter
the real.

To this end, the trickster masters of Zen embrace the absurd
and chase down the willing disciple. When you sign up for
this gig, you open yourself to all manner of harassment—from
sudden shouts in the ear to yanks of the nose to being picked
up and thrown off balconies. Zen masters are the champions
of poetic license: Any situation that might shake a disciple's
mind loose from its dreams is fair and honorable play.

One of Zen's most popular devices is the Zen stick. Origi-
nally, it was a literal stick—a heavy length of bamboo with
which masters stalked their disciples, hoping to catch them
unaware so that the Great Silence might dawn. Eventually the
literal stick gave birth to a subtler, figurative one, expanding
the master's range. Now he can hit with a word, a gesture, a
glance.

Literal or figurative, the rules of the game remain the same:
The disciple stumbles about unconsciously; the master stalks,
waiting for the precise moment to administer a good wop on

the head. Both master and disciple are victorious if the disciple's dreams are shattered before he takes his last fall.

Zen: a strong, full-bodied word, one that needs no other words framing it. The story is told of a certain Zen master who, when approached on the beach and asked to explain the meaning of Zen, picked up a stick and wrote in the sand: "ZEN." When the questioner asked if the master could elaborate on his answer, the master took up the stick again and wrote in much bigger letters: "ZEN."

The word seems to have come into being as "Dhyan," the Hindi word for meditation, migrated from India through China, where it became "Chaun"; and then to Japan, where it became "Zen." Let's listen to this sparse Japanese meditation:

Z—a wondrous sound. Our alphabet goes out with a zap, not a whimper. Zip-A-Dee-Doo-Dah, we are in the land of celebration, full of surpriZe!

And so, Zen zips in unexpectedly and opens us. Without warning, our nose is yanked, our head struck, our entire body thrown off the balcony: e! Our little ego lost in space, we respond with a cry of angst: "e!"

But just before we engage the mind to verbalize further protest, we suddenly notice how quiet it is. Quiet enough for the master's eyes to finally reach us, telling us to go inside now: n-n-n. Be still and know.

Zen.

But if this is not enough, if we are still stubborn in our somnambulant drift through life, the master will use his stick. There is an allegory in Zen that describes the varying needs of students: Some horses need to be struck with a whip, others need only to see the whip, while still others respond merely to the shadow of the whip. These gradations hold true for the Zen stick: While some only need to see its shadow, most of us need, from time to time, to feel its weight. Or at the very least, to hear its sound as it rushes toward us.

Stick. S-s-s. The sound an arrow makes as it speeds through the air, reaching its mark with the definite sound of t. S-s-sT!

The receiver of the hit responds with I!, a startled sound, a spine-straightening sound: I! And if the hit has done its work, the one on the receiving end is no victim; he turns and gives warning from the back of his mouth cave: ck! The master has fooled him out of timidity.

Standing straight, CKourageous, *and ready, he can receive the gift,
the present, the here and now.*

Consider this: Perhaps the Zen master's chasing around after
his beloved disciple is only a metaphor, a dramatization of
the antics that are always going on between us humans and
Existence. Perhaps this is the gig we have all signed up for, and
the universe has posted representatives at every corner of our
lives, each armed with a Zen stick.

To illustrate, here are three suspects from my life: one in
which the Zen master was a wild, red-haired, young woman
with a motorcycle; one in which the master was a thief; one in
which she was a child.

Lillian: Young Woman with a Harley

She was Brazilian with flaming red hair and smoldering eyes;
even before she got to know you, she grabbed your hand as
she spoke, gave passionate hugs, laughed out loud. She had
purchased a motorcycle—a Harley—and was heading out for
the Unknown as soon as spring semester was over. She wanted
to feel the wind in her hair and live out of a backpack, to find
what the world could be if she met it head-on, on her own
terms.

I was working as a student intern at the University Counseling Center when Lillian danced into my office, and my life. She
was eagerly responding to a call for experimental subjects for
my thesis research on creativity, which involved participating
in a sensory-awareness training group that my husband Terry
and I ran together, and taking a battery of creativity and percep-
tual tests before and after.

A flirtation soon sprouted between Terry and Lillian. Strange
as it may seem, even as I smelled the romantic fragrance flowing
between them, it was difficult to get too riled. Beneath a tart
skin of jealousy, I tasted a sweetness for Lillian. I loved her as
an image of myself, of what I might become if I broke free.

It was very late one night and I was in the computer room
entering my research data. I had decided to codify the subjects'

names by combining the first two letters of the first name and the first two letters of the last name. This became an interesting process, alone in the light of the midnight oil. Often people's code names formed pronounceable sounds, sometimes even real words. For example, Carol Smith would be CASM; John Cook would be JOCO; Robert Henry would be ROHE.

When Lillian's code name appeared on the screen, I stopped in my typing tracks. There, in all capital letters, stood her secret. Hidden in Lillian Fernandes was—LIFE.

Hari, the Thief

On one visit to India, I was robbed twice in the first month of my stay. As luck would have it, the ashram safe, where I usually kept my money, was temporarily closed, so I had stashed several hundred dollars and several hundred rupees in the drawer under my bed until I might decide where to keep it on a more permanent basis.

One night, upon returning to my flat, I found the door open. On the floor in the hallway, I came across the padlock beside a fat piece of wire that appeared to have been used in picking it. When I entered my room, I gasped. The drawer beneath my bed was upside down, with my clothing strewn all over. My money belt was lying there amidst the chaos, empty of the money, of course—all the money I had in the world at the time.

I rode out the initial hurricane of tears and shudders until I could manage to bicycle back to the ashram to share my horror with my best friend, Veeten. He immediately offered me some rupees. In fact, by the time I returned to my flat that night, I had received several gifts from friends and seemed to be financially afloat once more.

But several nights later, before I had found time to replace the padlock, I came home to a picked lock and the flat in shambles again. This time my only luxury possessions—a Sony Walkman with speakers and a small selection of tapes—were gone.

Although a bit of guilt was now added to insult and injury—after all, I did have fair warning about the flimsy lock—I somehow survived even this crisis. I had my locks changed and went on with my rather enchanted daily life at the ashram . . . until I arrived home one evening to find a note taped to my door: "The property that was stolen from this flat is waiting for your reclaiming at the police station." An address and "timings" (hours of business) were given at the bottom of the note.

The next day I went to the police station and presented my note to the uniformed man at the reception desk. He led me down long dark corridors and out the back door to a small, one-room, stone building at the back of the compound.

There were two policemen in the room—one behind the desk, the other standing at the door—and a small figure huddled in a blanket at the far corner. I assumed the person beneath the blanket to be a crime victim—probably a woman—momentarily taking shelter with the police.

The officers asked me to take a seat and offered me some *chai* (Indian spiced tea with milk). They were very cheerful, having a busy day with many Westerners coming by to reclaim stolen property.

"How did you know which houses to contact? Did the thief tell you?" I asked as I sipped my *chai*. I was curious how this whole thing came to pass. In all my years of knowing victims of robbery, and occasionally being one, I had never heard of anyone having their stolen goods returned.

Now the figure beneath the blanket moved and exposed a young Indian man's face. Without hesitation he said, "I told them. I am the thief."

I was shocked more at the thief's unapologetic directness than his confession, and turned to face him.

"There was money, too . . . ," I began.

"Yes," he said and went on to recall the exact amount, both rupees and dollars. "But all of that is spent," he said, "for Brown Sugar (heroin). . . . It is a terrible thing, but I will try to pay you back one day."

The police pressed on with their business of filling out forms. "What exactly did you lose?" the one behind the desk asked me.

"One Sony Walkman, two speakers, headphones. . . ."

"Any tapes?"

"Yes, tapes."

"How many?"

"Um . . . let's see . . . maybe eight, maybe ten . . ." I tried to count them in my mind.

"Thirteen," the small blanketed figure at my side said confidently.

I turned to him again as his clarity and willing participation intrigued me more and more.

"How did this come to pass, your returning my things?" I asked him.

"Things were getting hotter and hotter." His English was impeccable; he was much more articulate than even the police. "I knew this game was going to be over soon, so I turned myself in. . . ." Then he added once again, "If I had the money, I'd return it. For that, you will have to wait. If you put in a good word to the judge for me, perhaps you will get your money back sooner."

I nodded in acknowledgment of his tale and plea, though I couldn't imagine ever getting the money back.

"I'm Hari," he introduced himself, extending his small brown hand.

"I'm Prartho," I replied, taking his hand, feeling strangely pleased to make acquaintance with my thief.

Now he offered some personal advice. "The padlock at your flat is terrible."

"I know," I said, "I finally got around to changing it."

"Yes," he answered with a light laugh, "the new one's no better."

The police asked a few more questions before they were called away for a moment. As soon as they were out of earshot, Hari leaned toward me and asked, "Can you give me some money for *beedies* (Indian cigarettes, rolled in tobacco leaves)?"

Now, this was too much. Suddenly I was indignant and took advantage of my superior position, being the "free one," sitting on the chair.

"So now the thief turns to beggar?" my words came from on high.

Hari did not flinch. He looked at me with the same calm,

clear eyes and said, "There is a difference between begging and asking . . . I am asking."

I stopped to take a better look into his eyes and, indeed, it was so. These were not the eyes of a beggar. In fact, this was something I rarely encountered. Here was someone who was taking responsibility for himself.

Without another word, I went into my bag and pulled out a twenty-rupee note, which I gave him.

As soon as the policemen returned, Hari presented the rupees to one of them, speaking to him in Hindi, presumably putting in his *beedie* order. The officer looked at me, questioning. After all, the money could only be from me.

I smiled meekly and shrugged.

I knew it looked ridiculous, giving the man who had taken all my money a little more. But what could I do? I felt blessed to have met him.

Ami, the Child

In the large commune where I lived and worked, I had a cleaning job that included babysitting for the kindergarten through second-graders after school. The expectation was that we were to include the children in the cleaning, which was one of the greatest challenges I encountered during my years in the commune.

Ami was a six-year-old girl who was in my charge every afternoon. Her mother was Japanese, her father German, which resulted in a small-framed Oriental-looking child with feet planted firmly on the ground. Without a self-conscious bone in her body, she never hesitated to ask the most personal questions. She was my most willing cleaner.

Most every day, as soon as the children gathered, Ami grabbed a different playmate and volunteered to clean a bathroom. The first day I went to check on her work, she and the playmate were sitting in the bathtub in their underwear with soap bubbles climbing the walls around them, oozing over the rim of the tub, creeping across the floor.

"Oh no!" I shouted. "That's too much soap! This will take forever to rinse. . . ."

Ami stared up at me through her wide, almond eyes, jaw slightly open, expression deadpan. At last she said, "Cleaning is supposed to be fun, you know."

Recognizing the wisdom in this, I decided to forever leave Ami to her own devices, checking on her only occasionally—for inspiration purposes.

One afternoon Ami came into the bathroom, where I was cleaning. I was in a funk that day, complaining about anything I could find—and actively looking! For cleaners, complaining possibilities are a fringe benefit. How easy it is to walk into a room and begin sighing and chanting: "Disgusting, disgusting . . . look at this filth."

Gaining momentum with every spilt blob of toothpaste and every stray clump of hair, I was deep into the "Disgusting Chorus" when Ami came in. She said she wanted to say hello. And to use the toilet.

As I continued to be pleasantly grossed-out by every out-of-place item I could find, Ami sat there humming a little tune. Suddenly she blurted out, "I think *everything* is good."

"You do?" I turned to her incredulous, holding a pair of dirty socks between reluctant thumb and index finger, as far from my nose as possible.

She gave me that openmouthed, deadpan look again, and her smooth little-girl features melted into the weathered face of an ancient Zen master. "You mean you *don't?*" the master asked.

As if awakened from a dream, I looked into those fiercely innocent eyes and wasn't so sure. The dingy little room I had defined as life began to lighten and expand.

Now the figure on the toilet faded back into a little girl. She took to humming again, came to the sink to wash her hands, and skipped off—leaving me holding the dirty socks in a brand-new light.

Postscript

Albert Einstein has long been a hero of mine. I find his disheveled look endearing: those star-gazing eyes beneath the wild mop of hair, that expression of helplessness over his daring to see what everybody else refused to. I understand that his first insights about light and speed came to him in a dream when he was twelve years old, that his theory of relativity fell on him as he relaxed in the shade of a tree on a sunny day, that he mused about using only ten percent of his brain's intelligence. He was a man of subjective intelligence, trusting his own experience.

Einstein first caught me when I came across his perspective on the Divine: "God is subtle," he said. And in this, I felt the truth that if we are to meet the Almighty, we must stop our panicked rush for the Great Experience and pay attention to the very small.

Yesterday I found this quote of Einstein's on miracles: "There are only two ways to live your life. One is as though nothing is a miracle. The other is as if everything is."

Yes.

Perhaps the Universe is always—and only—up to this one trick: stalking us and hitting us again and again in hopes that we will awaken to the only miracle there is: *being alive.*